"You'd better explain yourself," Justin said

His voice was low, his tone dangerous.

It shocked Kelly for a moment, the electric contact of his touch...the frightening sense of being captured by him...the impact of his sudden closeness. Kelly's reaction was all the more intense because of it.

"Let go of me," she blazed, then plunged on recklessly, desperate to repel him and his confusing effect on her. "I can't trust myself to touch you any longer. I want to rip you apart for what you've done."

"What have I done?" His eyes narrowed. He released her wrist and propped himself up with an air of suffering patience. "Go ahead," he invited grimly. "I see you're bursting to enlighten me."

EMMA DARCY nearly became an actress until her fiancé declared he preferred to attend the theater *with* her. She became a wife and mother. Later she took up oil painting—unsuccessfully, she remarks. Then, she tried architecture, designing the family home in New South Wales. Next came romance writing—"the hardest and most challenging of all the activities," she confesses.

Books by Emma Darcy

Don't miss any of our special offers. Write to us at the following address for information on our newest releases.

Harlequin Reader Service
901 Fuhrmann Blvd., P.O. Box 1397, Buffalo, NY 14240
Canadian address: P.O. Box 603,
Fort Erie, Ont. L2A 5X3

EMMA DARCY

the ultimate choice

Harlequin Books

TORONTO • NEW YORK • LONDON
AMSTERDAM • PARIS • SYDNEY • HAMBURG
STOCKHOLM • ATHENS • TOKYO • MILAN

Harlequin Presents first edition August 1990
ISBN 0-373-11288-2

Original hardcover edition published in 1989
by Mills & Boon Limited

CHAPTER ONE

THE MOMENT he heard of Henry Lloyd's death, Justin St John knew that he would buy Marian Park.

He had always admired quality. And if ever any place held the true and lasting essence of quality it was Marian Park.

He didn't need the estate agent to show him over the property—to tell him that it was one of the finest merino sheep stud-farms in Australia—to lead him around the magnificent gardens which had been planned and planted by Marian Lloyd sixty years before—to take him through each room of the grand old country mansion. Even if the whole place had been neglected for the last sixteen years—which it hadn't—Justin would have bought it, anyway.

He paused in the beautifully proportioned drawing-room and stared at the portrait above the fireplace. The pain of loss was still as sharp as if it had happened yesterday.

The agent interpreted Justin's fixed look as one of curious interest.

'Noni Lloyd, the old man's granddaughter,' he explained. 'Painted after her twenty-first birthday. She died a year later. Fell from a horse. I understand she was a very promising rider in show-jumping circles. Beautiful girl.'

'Yes,' Justin murmured, the word only just husking over the welling lump in his throat. He swallowed hard. She was so vividly alive on that canvas...the only woman he had ever loved. No one else before or since had ever matched up to Noni Lloyd. Justin no longer believed that anyone ever would. And he knew he would never settle for second best.

'The portrait would fetch a good price if you wanted to sell it,' the agent prattled on.

'No. It belongs there,' Justin said curtly, and forced himself to turn away rather than suffer any more unwelcome comments. His grey eyes were bleak and steely as he met the look of speculative enquiry on the agent's face. 'I would want everything to remain exactly as it is,' he stated in a flat monotone.

Noni would have hated Marian Park passing into the hands of strangers. If she had not died that day, they would have married, had children...and the family tradition would have gone on. It was something he could do for her: see that it was all kept intact...as she would have done...as they would have done together.

Justin was barely conscious of where they walked after the agent steered him out of the house. Memories kept flooding through his mind, and it took most of his concentrated will-power to drive them out and keep them at bay until he could be alone again.

They emerged from the pine forest that sheltered the gardens and there were the stables, straight ahead. The stables where he had last kissed Noni before she had started out on that fatal ride...

His step faltered for a moment, his left leg stiffening as if in conscious protest. Justin pushed himself on. If he intended to live here, he had to learn to live with everything. Perhaps there might come a day when he could put the nightmare to rest.

He deliberately forced himself to look down at Noni's practice field where it had happened. The sense of time reeling backwards shook his mind and heart when he saw the woman rider urging her horse over the jumps Noni had used: the gate, the combination, the single rail, the triple...

Noni... wheeling the big black stallion short to gain time, trying to set him into stride. The horse barely skimming the first jump, knocking the rail on the second, balking at the last moment... crashing into the third, throwing Noni... its leg broken... panicking... dangerous...

Justin had run with fear in his mouth and desperation driving his legs like pistons. And he would have reached Noni, would have been able to protect her, save her, but for that last split-second decision. Even now he didn't understand—would never understand—what made him choose the way he had.

'Mr St John, are you all right?'

A hand clutched his shoulder. Justin swayed slightly, his skin clammy, his bad leg almost giving way under him. He recollected himself with difficulty, and turned to the agent who was staring anxiously at him.

'A momentary indisposition.' He tried to stretch his mouth into a reassuring smile. 'I'm ready to continue.'

The agent frowned. 'Sure you don't want to return to the house?'

'Certain.'

He completed the inspection that the agent directed, but his leg was giving him hell and his face was pinched with the pain of it when they finally returned to their cars in the driveway. Justin didn't know why he had forced himself to go through with the whole tour. A sense of duty? Respect? Guilt that he had never come back to visit Noni's grandfather?

He wished he hadn't seen the woman rider.

Henry Lloyd had never attached any blame to him for Noni's death. The old man had visited him in the hospital, insisted that Justin had only done what anyone would have done in the circumstances. But Noni was dead...and the choice he had made still haunted him.

He turned decisively to the estate agent. 'Tell the executors I'll buy the place. Settlement to be completed as soon as possible...' He laid down the terms he wanted.

'That's the best decision you've ever made!' the agent crowed, unable to contain his satisfaction. 'At twenty-two million, you're almost stealing it.'

Justin sliced him with a grim smile. 'At twenty-two million, I expect to get precisely what I want. To the letter.'

He was prepared to pay for quality. It wasn't all that easy to come by. A woman like Noni, a place like Marian Park—they were rare things. And Justin St John knew that, when the chance came along to acquire something of rare quality, even the most minute hesitation could lose it for you. He was not about to lose Marian Park.

But there was one last thing he needed to know. It had to be settled before he took up residence here. 'The woman rider we saw practising jumps . . . who is she? Someone belonging to the estate?'

'A local lass,' the agent replied. 'She had an arrangement with Henry Lloyd to ride his horses. She doesn't work here.'

Justin's mouth set in grim satisfaction.

The matter did not require any diplomacy. It was clear cut. The woman would have to find some other sponsor.

There would be no more show-jumping at Marian Park. And no horse he owned would ever be ridden for that purpose again. Perhaps Henry Lloyd had wanted a living reminder of his granddaughter around him. Justin St John didn't.

And down on the practice field that Henry Lloyd had set up for his granddaughter so many years ago,

Kelly Hanrahan urged the big black stallion on to the next jump, unaware that a decision had been made that would inexorably alter the course of her life from that time onwards.

CHAPTER TWO

KELLY'S first impulse was to refuse. Point-blank!

A furious anger boiled through her brain. It put a volcanic edge on the outrage she had nursed for days. She wanted—very, very much—to tell Justin St John where he could go. And what he could do with his money! She felt no sympathy whatsoever for his pain. If he really needed physiotherapy, he could find someone else to do it for him. She was not about to lay one helpful hand on that...that tyrant!

'Miss Hanrahan?' the caller prompted at the other end of the telephone line. He had introduced himself as Justin St John's secretary. The new squire of Marian Park didn't waste his precious time chatting with any of the local people.

Kelly seethed, torn between her natural humanity that demanded she relieve the suffering of a human being, and the knowledge that Justin St John was *not* a human being!

Her teeth gritted in resistance as second thoughts forced her to acknowledge that it wasn't exactly ethical to refuse anyone an appointment. Not even Justin St John! Besides which, if she had him at her mercy, she could use the opportunity to tell him precisely what she thought of him.

But she was not going to play the role of lackey to anyone. If he wanted the relief she could give him, he could come crawling to her!

She injected a frosty dignity into her voice. 'Would you please explain to Mr St John that no matter what fee he offers me, I do not give private physiotherapy outside my office. I do not lug a specialist table around with me...'

'We can set up a suitable table for you here, Miss Hanrahan,' the secretary quickly interrupted. 'And if you need help with any other equipment, I'll come and fetch it in the van and return it for you.'

'Wouldn't it be simpler for Mr St John to come to the office himself?' Kelly sliced back, barely restraining an acid note of sarcasm.

'Miss Hanrahan, the problem is mainly in the hip-joint. From an old injury. Travelling is extremely painful for him,' he explained in a tone of sweet reasoning. 'I'm sure that, given good-will on both sides, we can come to some arrangement that will not put you out too much.'

Kelly fumed. 'Put out' hit the nail right on the head! Justin St John had refused her everything! He had refused to consider the arrangement she had had with Henry Lloyd. He had refused to allow her access to the horses she had been training for years. He had even refused to see her personally. Which was bad enough, but what he was doing to Grandpa was so mean, so cruel...

She tried to calm down. Uncle Tom reckoned they had a good case against Justin St John reclaiming

Grandpa's property. Uncle Tom might not be a smart city solicitor, but he was wily in the ways of the land. All was not lost, not by a long shot. Justin St John was about to get the biggest fight he had ever had in his smug, privileged life!

And some inner voice told her that if she was ever going to get close enough to tell him what she thought of him this was her best chance.

On the other hand, Uncle Tom—who, technically speaking, was not her uncle at all—had warned her and Grandpa not to speak to Justin St John. They were to leave the matter entirely in his hands. Personal confrontations wouldn't win them anything in a case of law.

But Kelly's intuition urged that a little straight speaking was precisely what Justin St John needed. He couldn't very well order her off the premises when he had asked her to come. And, while it might not help Grandpa's case, it couldn't do any harm. It would certainly do *her* a powerful lot of good to get a few things off her chest!

'Very well,' she said decisively. But her inner turmoil had wiped out all recollection of the caller's introduction. 'Er... I'm sorry, I don't recall your name.'

'Farley. Roy Farley,' he supplied with brightened haste.

'I'll bring my equipment with me. You have the table ready. Will five-thirty this afternoon suit Mr St John's convenience?' She smiled as she said that, but if Roy Farley had seen the smile he might have had second thoughts about securing her services. It was a long way from being a smile of servility. Or of mercy.

'Certainly, Miss Hanrahan. I do hope Marian Park is not too far out of your way?' he added enquiringly.

'Actually, it's very close to home, Mr Farley. Very close,' Kelly repeated with secret relish. Too close for comfort, as Justin St John would very shortly discover!

'Oh, that will work out well, then,' the secretary enthused, obviously thinking that any future physiotherapy sessions would be no trouble at all. 'We'll look forward to seeing you at five-thirty, Miss Hanrahan,' he added with satisfaction, and rang off. Mission accomplished.

Kelly found it difficult to concentrate on her work for the rest of the afternoon. Justin St John was like a festering wound that gave her no peace, but at least she could let some of the pus out when she saw him this evening. It might be short-lived solace, but if she could tear into his self-centred little world the exercise would be well worth while.

Best not to tell Grandpa where she was going or what she intended to do. It would only churn him up again to no good purpose. And tonight was his chess night with Judge Moffat. Grandpa was sure to lose if he was upset over Justin St John again. Besides which, the judge was on their side, and he might come up with something to aid them in their fight.

She telephoned home in good time to warn her grandfather that she would be working late and not to wait dinner for her. There was a pre-cooked casserole in the refrigerator, and all he had to do was reheat it in the oven. Her grandfather didn't question her. This last week he seemed to have sunk into an apathy that was even more worrying to Kelly than the outbursts of rage over Justin St John.

Henry Lloyd's death had hit her grandfather hard. 'It's no good any more without Henry,' he had grumbled last night. 'The judge is a fine old friend, but it's not the same. Henry should have outlived me the way he always reckoned he would.'

'You've still got me, Grandpa,' Kelly had pointed out, trying to cheer him up.

The weary sadness only settled more deeply. 'And what good am I to you, Kelly? Only a burden. A burden that should be put to rest.'

The grief and strain and stress they had suffered since Henry Lloyd's death were telling on both of them. Tears welled in Kelly's eyes. 'Then I'd be all alone. Please don't wish that on me, Grandpa.'

He had ended up comforting her, as he had been comforting her all her life. She couldn't remember her parents. She had been only two years old when their car had hit a kangaroo, gone out of control, and slammed into a tree at the side of the road. Her mother and father were killed instantly, but Kelly had survived uninjured. There had only ever been three important people in her life: Grandpa and Noni and Henry Lloyd.

Henry had been like a second grandfather to her, and Noni like a wonderful big sister. She hadn't had parents, either. Her mother and father had divorced and were living separate lives overseas, so Noni lived with her grandfather just as Kelly lived with hers. She had taught Kelly how to ride, and played with her, and given her special treats—and Kelly had worshipped her.

But Noni had gone first—when Kelly was seven years old—and for months afterwards she had trailed around Marian Park looking for her, not believing Noni had left them all and was never coming back. It was only many years later that Kelly realised how kind and patient Henry Lloyd had been with her. But Noni's death had left him lonely, too, and the closest of bonds had grown between them.

It had been hard at first to believe he was gone, too. There had been no warning. Not the slightest premonition from Henry himself. He really had intended to outlive Grandpa. He simply went to bed one night and died in his sleep.

And if Grandpa gave up and died on her now... a terrible hollowness burrowed through Kelly's stomach. She knew it had to happen some day, but she would never be ready for it. And Justin St John was going to pay for adding injury to Grandpa's grief, making him feel worse than he had to be, so depressed and miserable that he no longer wanted to live.

Kelly saw her last patient out of the door, tidied up the office, then carefully transported the inter-ferential and the ultrasound to the back seat of her car which was parked behind the building. She vowed that if her equipment got damaged in any way Justin St John would pay through the nose for it. But she didn't really expect any problem with it.

She returned to lock up and made a last-minute visit to the Ladies that served all the offices in the compact medical centre. Normally she was not over-concerned about her appearance, but it would be no normal meeting between her and Justin St John. She wanted to look cool, calm, composed and professional...to put him off guard before she attacked!

She pulled a brush through the thick length of her dark auburn hair, neatened the fringe that swept above the natural arch of her eyebrows, approved the sparkling light of battle in her wide green eyes, and added a dash of fresh lipstick for sheer female vanity.

She tucked the tailored white shirt more firmly into the navy blue tailored skirt, checked that her homi-ped navy sandals were shiny clean and there was no run in her tights, heaved a sigh to relieve her inner tension, then picked up her shoulder-bag and set off on her way.

Marian Park was seventeen kilometres from the township of Bowral, not a long drive and always a pleasant one for Kelly. The southern tablelands of

New South Wales had a relatively cool climate, and the country was green and lush at this time of year.

If it wasn't for Justin St John, she would be rushing home to exercise the horses, getting them into peak condition for the last show-jumping venue at Dapto before the Australian Grand Prix at Wentworth Park.

As a last resort, she had contacted as many people as she thought might be able to help her out of her dilemma. She had been offered a number of rides, but only on second-string horses. They gave her no hope of winning the points she still needed to put her into the World Cup. Not that she could go overseas and leave Grandpa alone now, anyway. That dream had died with Henry Lloyd.

But Justin St John had buried it!

To take her horses away from her was as unfair as taking Grandpa's property. Henry Lloyd had certainly bought the stallions and the mares. He had indulged her with everything she wanted, in order to follow in Noni's footsteps. But it was Kelly's own work with them that had increased their value to such an extent that, if Justin St John sold them and pocketed the proceeds himself, it would be downright robbery.

After she had won the blue ribbon on Rasputin at the Perth Grand Prix, the visiting Koreans had offered five times the price Henry had paid for him. And Rapunzel, the palomino mare, had attracted an equal offer from the Japanese. Lady of Shallot and Sir Galahad, her second-string horses, could easily fetch triple their initial cost. And no way could Kelly afford to buy any one of them.

Show-jumping was a rich man's sport. But it made no difference to Kelly's burning sense of injustice. Any fair-minded person would have offered her a deal. Something. Anything! But Justin St John's solicitor had left her no leeway to argue her case. She had not paid for anything: not the horses or saddles or horse-truck or vet fees or hay or any other tangibles. All the prize money she won had gone on entrance fees and travelling expenses.

But it still wasn't fair!

Kelly belatedly returned the waves of a few people as she passed through the village of Crooked Creek. She spotted Uncle Tom yarning to Judge Moffat outside the courthouse, and hoped the judge wouldn't notice her car going by. He might comment on it to her grandfather—although she hadn't really lied about working late!

If it was a good chess game they wouldn't gossip much, she argued to herself, and dismissed the niggle from her mind.

The last few kilometres sped by. Kelly slowed her old Toyota as the road entered the pine forest which enclosed and sheltered the gardens of Marian Park. The avenue was dark and shadowy, and it was like going through a tunnel to another world.

The beauty and artistry of the grounds surrounding the grand old mansion were unique in Australia. When Kelly had been little it had seemed like a fairyland: the terraces of emerald lawns, magnificent specimens of imported trees—ash, elm, maple, beech, the fascinating topiary work, sunken gardens, statuary, hidden ponds, the wistaria walk, the banks of azaleas and rhododendrons. So much to delight the eye everywhere one turned.

And nothing had changed over the years. Here it was as if time stayed still. Kelly half expected to spot Henry Lloyd chatting to one of the gardeners, but the timelessness was only an illusion. The Lloyd era was over at Marian Park.

Sadness dragged at Kelly's heart as she drew the car to a halt under the ivy-covered portico which stretched over the driveway. Suddenly she didn't want to get out and go inside the house that was now occupied by a stranger. Even as she fought down the feeling, the front door opened and a man started down the steps towards her.

Too young to be Justin St John, Kelly decided, and pushed herself out of the car.

'Miss Hanrahan?' he greeted her, looking slightly surprised.

She recognised the voice from the telephone. 'Mr Farley,' she replied with a nod of acknowledgement.

He was thirtyish, sandy-haired, blue-eyed, his face too weatherbeaten to be that of a city man, and he was dressed in the khaki work-drill clothes that went with the outdoors. He gave her a slightly crooked smile which lent a softening friendliness to his rugged features. He was not unattractive, but Kelly was in no mood to appreciate the looks of any man connected to the enemy.

'I was expecting someone older,' he said. 'But it's good of you to come.'

'I expect Mr St John to make it worth my while,' Kelly reminded him with some asperity. She opened the back door of the Toyota. 'Perhaps you would carry that inside for me,' she directed, indicating the interferential which was heavy and cumbersome to handle. And, since Roy Farley was obviously Justin St John's lackey, he might as well earn his keep!

'Of course,' he said, and treated the machine with conscientious care.

Kelly picked up her handbag and the ultrasound and followed him. She steeled herself to walk through the home that would never again be a second home to her. But apparently the new broom hadn't swept through the house yet. No changes had been made to any of the furnishings that she could see. Everything was exactly the same. Kelly wasn't sure if she felt relief or resentment.

It surprised her when she was led to the guest wing. A moment's consideration made her realise that Justin St John would not be using the stairs in his condition. She was ushered into a bedroom where two tables had been arranged for her: one for the equipment, the other draped with a large bath-towel.

'I trust this is satisfactory?' Roy Farley asked anxiously as he set the interferential down and plugged it into a power-point.

'It will serve,' Kelly replied.

He threw her a relieved smile, then knocked on the door to the adjoining bathroom. 'The physiotherapist is here, Justin,' he called.

'I'll be out in a minute.'

The voice was deep, with the cultured tone that was undoubtedly the built-in product of a high-class Victorian boarding-school. Kelly might have conceded that it was pleasant, if it had not belonged to the person she had most reason to hate.

'He's in the spa bath,' Roy Farley explained as he turned back to her. 'If there's nothing else you require, I'll leave you to it.'

'Thank you,' Kelly said dismissively.

She glanced at her watch as he left the room, sourly wondering how long Justin St John's minute would be. Not that it really mattered. She would have him just where she wanted him soon enough.

Conscious that her nerves were tightening now that the confrontation she had planned was imminent, Kelly busied herself plugging in the ultrasound and taking out the bottle of oil and box of tissues from her bag. When she heard the bathroom door click open, she carefully composed an expression of professional detachment and slowly swung around.

Kelly did not know if her look of detachment remained intact. For some immeasurable length of time her brain didn't register anything but the image of the man who stood in the bathroom doorway. He was tall and tanned and impressively male; all the more so since he wore only a brief pair of underpants. There was nothing soft about him, and his utter stillness seemed to intensify the power of his presence.

His hair was straight and black, thick and slightly spiky from the bath steam. The harsh planes of his face converged to give him a strikingly individual look that was compelling rather than handsome, feral rather than civilised. The dimple in his chin was almost incongruous, yet it added an intriguing spice to his strong animal-like quality. His eyes were deeply set and slate-grey: hard and uncompromising and intensely concentrated on her.

Kelly felt a nerve-tingling sense of familiarity, as if she had seen him somewhere before. But that wasn't possible. There had been no photograph with the fulsome biography which had been printed in the local newspaper. He had been a business leader in Sydney for the last fourteen years. Prior to that, he had lived on the vast and prosperous St John sheep property in Victoria. In his youth he had been a polo player of international standard—one of the very few with a top ten-goal handicap—until an accident had disabled him. Kelly had never moved in polo-playing circles.

However, one question was now answered. She understood why his orders were obeyed to the letter. Few men would have the nerve to stand up to him. He exuded a raw power that challenged anything and anyone, asserting by nature that victory would be his. Other people's lives might be determined by forces outside themselves, but Kelly felt certain that this man would always determine his own fate.

For one weak moment she quailed at the prospect of taking him to task for what he had done, but a fiery sense of righteousness burned up her spine, stiffening her backbone and tilting her chin with stubborn pride. No way was she going to bend her head to his might! He might beat her, but she was not going to be cowed by him. Never!

Kelly wasn't aware of the signals emanating from her—the aggressive lift of her chin, the perceptible tightening of her full, sensual lips, the slight flush that marked her delicate cheekbones, the sudden glitter of battle-readiness in the darkly fringed green eyes—but every nerve in her body bristled as Justin St John's mouth took on a sardonic twist.

'I wasn't expecting a girl. I've never had one before.'

Kelly burned at the condescension, and fiercely resented the strong sexuality he exuded. He was not young. She judged him to be about forty. But that only made him appear more dangerous. He was too knowing and experienced, and far too self-assured to be attackable from any angle. Nevertheless, she couldn't resist one gibe.

'You're lucky to get anyone, Mr St John. You're too much of a newcomer for your name to carry any weight around here. And your money isn't the answer to everything,' she said acidly.

Kelly rued the rash words the moment they were out. They seemed to hang in the air between them for endless seconds, and her pulse did a panicky jig at the sharpened glint of speculation in his eyes. With slow deliberation he shook his head, as if he was mocking her or himself.

'You are very young,' he said flatly. 'But you're obviously qualified or you wouldn't be here.'

'Don't worry!' she shot back. 'You'll get the treatment you need.' *And deserve*, Kelly added privately. 'Can you manage to get up on the table by yourself?'

His face stiffened at her taunt. 'I'll manage,' he asserted grimly.

But it obviously pained him to walk. He moved his left leg stiffly, cautiously, and when he finally settled himself on the table he breathed a sigh of relief. Quite clearly he had favoured one leg for years. It was not so powerfully muscled as the other.

'You'd better tell me the whole story, so I don't get anything wrong,' Kelly said matter-of-factly.

'My left side was smashed from the waist down. The bones didn't knit properly. There's a lot of pain in the joints. The problem area just now is between hip and thigh.'

Kelly grimaced to herself. She didn't like feeling any sympathy for the enemy, but she could not bring herself to completely ignore his suffering. She had to do something about it.

'I'll start with the ultrasound,' she decided.

He nodded.

Delicately she moved his underwear away from the joint and spread oil over his taut flesh. The touch of him was oddly disturbing. Repugnant, she told herself, but knew she was shading the truth. His body was that of a superb athlete and, despite his disablement, he was in sleek condition. Her touch seemed to disturb him, too. She could feel his flesh flinching under her hand.

'Is that hurting?'

'No,' he growled.

'How did you get smashed up?' she asked, covering her unease with ordinary curiosity.

'That's irrelevant,' he answered curtly.

Kelly tried to repress her irritation over his rudeness. She turned away, using unnecessary vigour in wiping the oil from her hand with tissues before plugging in the ultrasound and switching it on. The small machine was shaped much like a Philips electric razor and about the same size. She began to move it over the joint and muscles.

'If you feel any heat, tell me,' she instructed.

'Get on with it,' he growled impatiently.

Kelly threw him a venomous look. Fortunately his eyes were closed. His whole face had a closed, tight look. Kelly decided to give him ten minutes with the ultrasound.

She couldn't remember ever seeing a more... interesting male body.

He made no sound.

She worked on in silence until the automatic timer clicked off. Then, having wiped the oil from his skin with a few tissues, she fixed the suction cups on to his body: two red, two blue. 'I'm going to switch the interferential on now. Tell me when the pins and needles start.'

'Give it to me full blast.'

You'll get it full blast, Kelly silently promised him...after she had finished the job. She turned the dials.

He made no sound.

She saw the muscles around his hip joint start to contract. 'That's far enough,' she said.

He grunted.

Ten minutes would be long enough for the first treatment, she thought. It would probably also be the last...from her!

It seemed to be only justice that some defect had been inflicted on him. Something to cut his superiority down!

Kelly took grim satisfaction in imagining him as the self-centred type who would never give enough of himself to make a relationship work. A sexy body was all he would ever offer. And he'd consider that the woman who shared a bed with him for a while was positively privileged to have the honour.

Kelly had experienced that before. When she had been at Cumberland College she had been naïve enough to fall for a handsome face. But once bitten, twice shy. The sexiest guys were always egotistic and self-centred and didn't care how they hurt you. The nice guys were totally unexciting. How on earth was a girl to find someone just right?

She stared resentfully at the body stretched out in front of her. It certainly wasn't fair for Justin

St John to have everything: looks and wealth and Marian Park and her horses and Grandpa's land!

Kelly's rage boiled up again. She switched off the interferential and removed the suction cups. She didn't feel like going on with the treatment, but she had principles to live up to even if Justin St John didn't!

'I'm going to do mobilisations on the hip-joint,' she informed him. 'Tell me when the pain gets bad.'

'How do you measure pain?' he rumbled.

'Imagine a scale from one to ten. How does this feel?' She pushed into the warm flesh of his left buttock, finding the top of the femur.

He grunted. 'One!'

She pushed down harder.

'You've just zoomed up to five,' he gasped.

She eased back a little. The inclination to throw her whole weight on to him was almost irresistible. 'How's that?' she bit out, thinking of her grandfather's misery and her bitter frustration over the horses.

'Better!' he croaked.

But the temptation to push on was a malevolent cloud on her mind. She pressed down a bit harder. He groaned. It was then that Kelly knew she couldn't go on. She really did want to hurt him. Horrified at her own driven urge to cruelty, she snatched her hands away from him.

He looked back at her in surprise.

'I can't! I just can't!' she cried, appalled and distressed that she could be tempted into taking such a dreadful advantage of anyone, no matter how vengeful she felt. 'That's the end of it!' she snapped, all the more angry with him because she was so upset with herself. 'If it wasn't against my own personal ethics, I'd give you every measure of pain there was, Justin St John! You deserve every bit you get. But I'm not as callous as you, so you can just go on suffering by yourself.'

His eyes were wide open now, sharply alert and diamond-hard. His arm shot out and a vice-like hand fastened around Kelly's wrist. 'You'd better explain yourself,' he said in a low, dangerous tone.

It shocked her for a moment, the electric contact of his touch . . . the frightening sense of being captured by him . . . the impact of his sudden closeness. Kelly's reaction was all the more intense because of it.

'Let go of me!' she blazed, then plunged on recklessly, desperate to repel him and his confusing effect on her. 'It's not exactly hard to work it out, is it? I can't trust myself to touch you any longer. I want to rip you apart for what you've done.'

'What I've done?' His eyes narrowed. He released her wrist and rolled on to his right side, propping himself up on his elbow with an air of suffering patience. 'I see you're bursting to enlighten me, so go ahead,' he invited, his mouth taking on a grim curve. 'This is your chance. Maybe it's the last you'll ever have.'

CHAPTER THREE

KELLY folded her arms, needing to wipe away the feeling his hand had branded on her wrist, but not wanting to be conspicuous about it. She fixed Justin St John with a baleful glare and chose her words with bitter precision.

'The name Hanrahan apparently means nothing to you, Mr St John. You either don't know, or you don't care. But my grandfather and I are the so-called tenants that you wish to evict from our home. A home, I might add, that was built by my grandfather and his father almost seventy years ago. And which has been occupied continuously by our family ever since.'

She paused for that information to sink in, but there was not even a flicker of reaction on Justin St John's face. His expression might have been carved from granite. His gaze returned hers with the steadiness of a rock.

'It was presented to me that there were tenants on property that belonged to Marian Park. That they were freeloaders who were not paying any rent,' he stated flatly.

Blind fury overwhelmed her. She would have hit him if she had been a man. 'How dare you talk of my family like that?' Outrage almost choked her. 'Rent?' she spat out. 'Freeloaders?' she shrieked.

Her hands flew out in vehement dismissal of his argument, and the blazing green daggers of her eyes sliced viciously at Justin St John. 'My family has always paid its way! Always! Of course there wasn't any rent—Henry Lloyd would have scorned to take Grandpa's money. Henry Lloyd was a gentleman...'

'You are not making any sense,' he cut in impatiently.

'You want sense?' she shouted at him. 'I bet you had baked lamb for dinner last night. Or grilled lamb. Or lamb stew. Or something lamb!'

'Yes, but...' He sighed in resignation. 'What has that got to do with anything?'

'Where do you think it came from?' she yelled at him triumphantly.

'I have no idea.'

'From Grandpa! You eat his food. You don't mind taking our best fat lambs, do you? But then you break every agreement ever made. You threaten Grandpa with eviction. What are you trying to do? Kill him?'

He frowned. 'What is this agreement? What are you talking about?'

'The agreement between us and Marian Park, that's what! And you haven't heard of it because you wouldn't listen. But you'll listen now, by heaven! The agreement was never put on paper, but my great-grandfather and Henry Lloyd's father shook hands on it. That was all that was necessary. They were men. Men's men! Not like you!'

Her chin lifted with stormy pride. 'They fought side by side in the trenches of the Somme during the First World War. And helped each other survive the terrible conditions and hardships. They forged a friendship that crossed all barriers of wealth and class. And the word "gentleman" did mean something in those days!'

The vivid green eyes flashed her scorn at him. 'You might have the wealth to buy Marian Park. And you certainly have the arrogance to think you have class! But you'll never belong here. Not in a hundred years! You're not gentleman enough to clean Henry Lloyd's boots! You set yourself up as lord of the manor, and don't even bother to find out whom you're trampling over.'

'What was the gentleman's agreement you refer to?' he demanded to know. His voice was even, but there was now a glitter in his eyes that suggested she had struck a nerve.

Danger prickled down Kelly's spine as she remembered Uncle Tom's warning. Maybe she had gone too far. 'Our solicitor is dealing with that. The point is...that parcel of land belongs to Grandpa. He cleared it, fenced it, worked it and built it up. Everyone in Crooked Creek will attest to that. He might not have legal title to it at the moment, but don't think we'll stand by and let you take it away from us. We'll fight you every inch of the way.'

Justin St John moved. Kelly instinctively stepped back, then berated herself for cowardice. He might be strong and threatening, but she had right on her side and she wasn't going to budge until he had heard her out. She placed her hands on her hips in a belligerent pose.

He eased his legs over the edge of the table and sat up, grimacing at the pain it cost him to do so. There was a tired sickness in the eyes that swept up to hers again, but Kelly stubbornly ignored the stab of sympathy she felt.

'Miss Hanrahan...' His mouth took on an ironic twist. 'You're quite exceptionally beautiful when you're angry.'

She flushed with indignation. 'Don't think you can soft-soap me!'

'No. Perhaps not.' He gave a thin smile. 'You have the advantage over me. Could you bring yourself to oblige me with your first name?'

'Kelly. Kelly Hanrahan,' she answered proudly.

'Very Irish.'

Kelly instantly bridled at the comment. 'Yes!' she snapped, remembering his family history from the newspaper article. A St John had been a marine captain in the First Fleet in 1788. Eventually he had been granted land in the new colony. The St Johns of this world had always had it far too easy. It infuriated her further that this St John thought he could lord it over her.

'We came out here during the potato famine of 1848, when the English left us to starve in our millions. They don't have much of a record of treating the Irish fairly, do they?' she taunted.

'That was a long time ago.'

'You're still inflicting pain!'

He eyed her consideringly. 'It would seem my solicitor has been over-zealous in carrying out my orders,' he said with measured deliberation. 'I told him I didn't want tenants and to handle the legal problems involved, and to buy out all the leases. I did not realise, nor was I told, the circumstances pertaining to this matter. I'll order a report on the situation tomorrow. Does that satisfy you?'

'That you order a report?' Kelly whipped back at him scathingly. 'Of course I'm not satisfied! You're killing my grandfather, and you want to fob me off with a promise to look into it?' She looked at him with utter contempt. 'You wealthy people are totally unscrupulous!'

'Why should I trust your word?' he countered, his eyes hardening into steely cynicism. His gaze flicked down to her feet and up again with deliberate provocation. 'I'm too old to be easily taken in by a beautiful face and a delectable body. I know no more about you than what you've told me. Why should I believe you? What if you're just acting this out?'

'Oh! Oh…' Momentarily robbed of speech, Kelly stamped her foot. Then, absolutely steaming with outrage, she turned her back on him and stomped over to the window. She stared blindly out at the croquet lawn, tears of frustration burning her eyes.

She should have known it was no use speaking to him. Uncle Tom had told her.

'Kelly...' The unexpectedly soft intonation of her name sent a queer little shiver down her spine. 'If what you say is true, a little time for me to investigate is not unreasonable.'

She clenched her hands and whirled on him. 'If you were reasonable, you would have investigated in the first place, instead of...' To her intense mortification, tears rushed into her eyes. 'My grandfather doesn't have a lot of time!' she stormed over the lump in her throat. 'He's eighty-four years old and he doesn't have the... the will to keep going any more. That's what you've done to him with your damnable... damnable...'

She took a deep breath to steady her quivering lips, and smeared the tears away with a quick swipe of her hand, no longer caring what Justin St John thought of her. She was determined to speak out even if it was futile.

'It was terrible when Henry Lloyd died. He and Grandpa had been such close friends all their lives. They'd shared each other's joys and griefs all these years. And Henry Lloyd always wagered that Grandpa would die first, that he'd outlive him by a decade or two...'

Her voice hardened into bitter accusation. 'Then you come and take the heart out of him. What was left of it. One killing blow after another. The shock of having his home threatened on top of the grief of losing Henry. The stress of having to go to the solicitors. Henry Lloyd would turn in his grave if he knew. You're a no-good...' She was lost for words to describe him.

And he wasn't listening, anyway. He seemed to be staring straight through her. There was a frozen look about his face, as if he had completely withdrawn to another time and place.

Hopelessness dampened the rebellious fire that had driven her so far. It had all been a waste of time and energy coming here. She forced herself to move back to the table which held her equipment. There was nothing she could do but pack up and go.

'What is your grandfather's name? His full name?'

'What does it matter?' she muttered resentfully, ignoring him as she put the oil and tissues back in her bag.

There was a slight rustle of cloth as he pushed himself off the table. A hand closed around her arm and swung her around to face him. The impact of him—so near, so threateningly male in his seminakedness—tripped her heart and caught the breath in her throat.

'Tell me!' he commanded, taking hold of her other arm in an imprisoning and punishing grip.

Her pulse leapt in wild agitation, but a surge of defiance forced her to meet his eyes in angry challenge. Yet something in their expression—a pained, haunted look—startled her into answering him.

'It's Michael. Michael O'Reilly.' Her voice came out husky, strange to her own ears.

He closed his eyes and shook his head. He withdrew one hand from her to rub at his eyelids with finger and thumb. 'I'm sorry,' he said on a note of deep regret. 'I didn't think . . . it's so long ago . . .'

The last words were expelled on a ragged sigh, and Kelly didn't know what to make of them. Nor did she think to ask. The play of emotion on Justin St John's face held her mesmerised. She had judged him as unfeeling, yet she found herself caught up in the pain that emanated from him.

He dropped his hand to her shoulder as his eyes opened, and they were the washed grey of a bleak winter, shadowed by dark elements that instantly encompassed her and struck a quivering uncertainty in her heart. His fingers squeezed a light reassurance, but she didn't feel reassured. He was a stranger to her, yet somehow . . . they were not the hands of a stranger.

'I am sorry to have caused you both so much distress,' he said in obviously sincere apology. 'I was . . . preoccupied with other things and neglected to check on what was happening.' He grimaced, then took a deep breath. 'Tell your grandfather . . . assure him that I will not contest his ownership of the portion of Marian Park that he has always occupied. I will instruct my solicitor to give him legal title to it so that no question about possession will ever arise again. However, should either he or you ever wish to sell, I would like first option to buy.'

She stared at him blankly, not believing the words he had said, looking for the trick, looking for the lie.

His mouth tilted. 'Is that enough? What more can I do?'

'It's unbelievable,' she whispered, bewildered by his about-face. 'Do you know my grandfather?'

'No. Not personally. A long time ago I had a connection with the Lloyd family. What you said about the relationship between your two families stirred a recollection. And I'd forgotten that your grandfather's name is not necessarily your own. I apologise again . . . for doubting you.'

His expression changed to one of whimsical tenderness. A glow of warmth dispersed the shadows in his eyes, and the harsh lines of his face smoothed and took on a boyish charm. 'You obviously love him very dearly.'

Again Kelly found herself oddly breathless. A feeling of pleasure tingled through her veins and her heart was pumping with extraordinary vigour. 'Yes,' she said in that husky voice that didn't seem to belong to her. 'My parents died when I was two years old, and Grandpa brought me up.'

'I see,' he murmured.

The hand on her shoulder slid to the curve of her neck and slowly curled around it. His thumb brushed down her jawline in a tingling caress. Kelly swallowed to counteract a sudden dryness in her throat. It was madness—absolute madness to think what she was thinking: he was nearly twice her age—she had hated him only a few minutes ago—and whatever was throbbing between them couldn't be what she thought it was.

A sense of shifting...to a complete understanding. That was what it had to be. A relaxation from all the emotion spent. A new appreciation of each other.

His gaze dropped to her mouth.

Her lips actually parted in anticipation.

Her heart thundered.

His head started to bend.

Madness, her mind screamed.

She closed her eyes tight and willed her mouth to speak. 'Please let me go.'

The words were hardly more than a whisper.

She heard his sharp intake of breath. The powerful link—whatever it was that had bound them together in those few electric seconds—was broken even before he withdrew his physical hold on her. She was aware of a sharp, bereft feeling in herself. Her eyes flicked open in the quest for understanding, but she caught only a fleeting glimpse of tearing conflict on his face before he turned away from her.

'I'll call Roy to come and carry your equipment out for you,' he said in curt dismissal, and walked stiffly to the table, where he picked up a telephone and punched a number on the house intercom.

Kelly suffered a rush of emotions that kept her tongue-tied as he spoke to his secretary. Embarrassment that she might have misread his intentions was uppermost. Her own reaction to him didn't bear thinking about. Shame squirmed through her. She had been so wrong about him. He was being more than fair with Grandpa. And she had said such dreadful things...

He replaced the telephone and threw her a tight, bleak look. 'He'll be right down. If you'll excuse me...'

'Wait!' she cried as he stepped towards the bathroom.

She sensed his reluctance, but he turned to face her. All the harsh lines were back—no boyish charm now. His expression was one of cold, tight reserve, and the tension emanating from him almost strangled her vocal cords.

'I'm sorry for having thought so badly of you,' she croaked.

'That's immaterial now, Miss Hanrahan. I will have the title papers delivered to your grandfather. Please don't come back here again.'

'But...' His hardline rejection of any more personal communication between them was shocking and surprisingly hurtful. 'You haven't let me thank you,' she finished limply.

'I don't need to be thanked for doing what should have been done in the first place.'

Still she struggled against his edict, driven by a tumult of feelings that she didn't stop to define. 'The physiotherapy...I could come back tomorrow and...'

'No! I don't want you here!' he said savagely, and the flicker of revulsion on his face left her with no argument. It was all too plain that he didn't want her anywhere near him.

And she knew then... knew that he had wanted to kiss her, and was appalled at himself for having felt such a desire. He would rather suffer pain than be confronted with such a desire again.

And hadn't she herself known it was madness? Even worse madness to wish it had happened! Where could it possibly lead...to get mixed up with him?

A knock on the bedroom door broke the tension between them. Roy Farley entered and Justin St John waved him towards the equipment. 'We're finished,' he said, then limped into the bathroom and closed the door behind him without a backward glance.

Roy Farley handed Kelly a cheque for her professional services. It felt wrong to take it, but she shrank from facing the questions her refusal would inevitably raise, and she had given Justin St John some treatment. Nevertheless, guilt added more entanglement to her confused emotions as she packed up to leave.

Roy Farley carried the interferential out to the car. Kelly thanked him distractedly and climbed in behind the wheel. It wasn't until she was driving away that she realised she had said nothing about the horses.

CHAPTER FOUR

KELLY frowned over the unresolved problem, then shrugged it aside. She would tackle Justin St John about the horses another time. She had saved Grandpa from having to fight eviction. His land and home were now secured. That was the important thing! What Justin St John felt about her and what she felt about him...even the horses...they were pale considerations against what had been achieved.

Nevertheless, it was difficult to block out the mixture of emotions that Justin St John had evoked in her. He was certainly different from what she had expected. Different and...strangely compelling. She felt a distinct sense of loss at the way their meeting had ended.

But the loss was quickly counterbalanced by the surge of well-being she felt as she drove out of the pine forest and headed down the road that cut through the grazing pastures of Marian Park. This place was so much a part of her life that Kelly couldn't imagine belonging anywhere else. And now she never had to leave it. She drank in the scene around her with a heady sense of exhilaration.

The merino sheep that dotted the fields were the best in the world for their wool; descended from

Saxony and Silesian strains that could be traced back to the Escurial flocks of the Spanish kings, and the Rambouillets of Louis the Sixteenth, but now bred into a unique strain that was unequalled outside of Australia.

The whole national flock—over a hundred million sheep—had their genetic make-up determined by just twenty-one parent studs, of which Marian Park was undoubtedly the best—in Kelly's opinion. After all, how could it be less than the best when it could boast ownership of Octavian Augustus the Fourth, the cream of the industry's élite rams? Henry Lloyd had been offered a quarter of a million dollars for him, but no way would Henry have ever countenanced Octavian Augustus the Fourth's leaving Marian Park.

This was home to the prize ram. Just as it was home to her and Grandpa, even if that claim could only be made in a subsidiary sense. To be part of this property in any way at all was a matter of intense pride. Marian Park was real quality—one of the great stud sheep showplaces in the world—on a par with Haddon Rig and Falkiner's.

Of course, Grandpa's flock wasn't in the same class and was never meant to be. He was in the business of breeding fat lambs for eating. Merinos crossed with Border Leicesters or Romney Marshes were good producers. Sometimes he cross-bred with Corriedales because they combined fine mutton with a high class of wool. They all had their place in the sheep industry. And, of course, Marian Park always received the best from him.

That was how it had always been. And how it would now continue to be. The O'Reillys and Hanrahans kept their agreements.

Kelly smiled as their house came into view—their home for as long as they wanted it to be. It was nothing grand like the Lloyd mansion, but it was a good solid house in the Australian colonial style: white-painted weather-board, verandas all around, and a green corrugated iron roof with the bull-nosed eaves that were becoming fashionable again.

Grandpa would never have to leave it now, and Kelly felt a thrill of triumph at what she had achieved.

She zoomed through the gateway and didn't bother to drive down to the shed to put her car away. That could wait until later. She was eager to tell Grandpa the good news.

She pulled up beside Judge Moffat's car, raced up the front steps and burst into the kitchen where the two old men were still sitting over their dinner. 'Guess what I've done?' she cried, beaming her exhilaration at them.

Both men appeared too sunk in gloom to lift anything but glum faces to her. Although Kelly would have relished drawing out the news for its maximum impact, the need to inject some cheerful optimism had top priority. She related her confrontation with Justin St John and its happy outcome in as few words as possible, and had the pleasure of seeing ten years lift from her grand-father's face.

His surprise and relief gradually settled into a righteous satisfaction. His eyes sparked with new life, his sunken cheeks puffed out, his jawline firmed, and his shoulders lifted. He was no longer the impressive figure of a man he had once been, he had grown thin and wiry with age, and was almost bald, but the old strength of character rose out of the lines in his face and Kelly silently re-joiced in his rejuvenation.

'At least he's seen one of his mistakes!' Michael O'Reilly declared with ringing satisfaction.

'He actually said he would hand the title deeds over?' Judge Moffat questioned sharply, wary of accepting what Kelly had told them at face value.

He was a big man in his late sixties, florid of face and with a distinguished thatch of snow-white hair. His light blue eyes narrowed in speculative thought at Kelly's insistence that Justin St John had given her his solemn assurance.

'Well, I'd have to mark that in his favour—if he carries through on it—but I wouldn't be counting your chickens before they hatch, Michael,' he ad-vised her grandfather heavily. 'Not after what I heard from Tom Kennedy down at the courthouse this afternoon. Justin St John is very slippery. In my experience, a man like that cannot be trusted.'

'What did Uncle Tom say?' Kelly asked, con-fident in her own mind that Justin St John would keep his word.

'It's about the sheep,' her grandfather answered with a disapproving frown. 'The most terrible thing, Kelly! He's selling us out. He's selling the country out. He's selling everybody out.'

'A traitor! We've got to find a way to stop him,' the judge rumbled. 'If we don't, we're all going to lose a lot of money. The Russians won't even want to look at my rams, let alone buy them. He's a traitor, all right. A traitor to everyone!'

'What's going on? What's he done?' Kelly demanded impatiently, finding the accusation distinctly unpalatable.

Judge Moffat huffed. 'You know the government will only allow five hundred rams to be exported overseas each year...'

'Yes, of course. It's an enormous concession. Our wool per sheep is almost double the world average. Why should we give that advantage away?'

'Exactly! I don't mind selling them good sheep as long as we keep the best for ourselves. But Justin St John has found a way around it! He's sold us out!' the judge almost thundered in his indignation.

'How?' Kelly asked in bewilderment.

'The Russians are going to get Octavian Augustus the Fourth,' her grandfather answered mournfully.

Shock bounced around Kelly's mind. She refused to believe it. No one could be that mad. But her grandfather and Judge Moffat believed it. She groped for words in Justin St John's defence. 'That's impossible! He can't do it! Octavian Augustus the Fourth is the greatest merino ram in the world. The government would step in. They won't allow it.'

'That's the iniquity of the thing!' the judge growled. 'He's keeping Octavian Augustus the Fourth. He's selling the semen for artificial insemination...'

'But that's illegal!' Kelly pounced, relieved that they had to be wrong about Justin St John. For some reason that she didn't stop to examine, she didn't want to believe he was bad any more. 'You can't export it. It's against the regulations!' she said triumphantly.

'That's where he's so clever,' her grandfather put in with grudging admiration. 'Everyone in Crooked Creek will wish they'd thought of it first. He's going to be hated for it.'

'For what?' Kelly almost screeched.

'He's impregnating five thousand ewes. When they conceive, the ewes carry the embryos out of the country and there goes the breeding strain from Octavian Augustus the Fourth. He's already had the Russian ambassador down...'

'Should be hung, drawn, and quartered!' the judge thundered, clearly of the opinion that the statute books should still allow that particular sentence to be handed down. He threw up his hands in despairing appeal. 'How am I going to sell my rams to them when they get that standard of breeding over there? At the very least, it will depress prices abysmally!'

'But can he do it, Grandpa?' Kelly asked, feeling very confused about the man.

'Nothing to stop him that I know of. Or the judge. Australia needs the Russians to develop their wool industry to defeat the threat of synthetic fibre. Henry Lloyd told me that himself. And then there's the humanitarian side. Russia is one of the coldest countries in the world. It needs better, heavier wool to keep its population warm. But Justin St John is sure going to clean up with this deal. He'll make so much money...'

'Disgusting! Absolutely disgusting!' the judge cried in heartfelt condemnation.

Kelly only just managed to stifle a smile. Justin St John was certainly a smart operator, and he might be revolutionising the industry, but he wasn't doing anything bad in selling the ewes to the Russians.

And it was now perfectly clear that the judge, who owned a daughter stud, fiercely resented the fact that he hadn't thought of the scheme first.

Naturally Grandpa sympathised with him. Justin St John had been the enemy up until tonight, and it would take a little while to readjust that thinking.

'Well, at least we're going to keep this place,' she said brightly, wanting to remind her grandfather that the shadow had lifted from their future.

'Don't believe anything until you have the title deeds in your hands,' the judge grumbled pessimistically.

But her grandfather looked more spry than he had for weeks as he rose from the table and suggested they adjourn to the living-room for their chess game. And some three hours later, after he had waved the judge goodnight, he boasted to Kelly that he had wiped his friend off the board with one checkmate after another.

All in all, it had been a victorious night.

Kelly set off for work the next morning in buoyant spirits. Her grandfather had eaten a good breakfast and was out looking over his sheep, which clearly demonstrated a healthy interest in life. It was the interferential on the back seat of the Toyota which reminded her that their benefactor of last night was probably facing the day with more pain than pleasure.

Justin St John was certainly suffering from the old injury to his leg, and the physiotherapy she had given him would only have effected minimum relief. Judging from the pain he had been unable to hide, Kelly reckoned he needed daily treatments for at least a week before the trouble would really ease. Probably a fortnight. After what he had done for her and Grandpa, Kelly wanted to help him. But would he let her?

His refusal of her offer last night had been so emphatic, she could hardly ignore it. He couldn't have been more adamant that he did not want her to come back to Marian Park. But surely that was just an extreme reaction to what had only been— a momentary aberration on both their parts.

Certainly he had a very masculine attraction—Kelly couldn't deny that—and she was not unaware that most men gave her a second look, although to say she was beautiful was stretching the truth, and she viewed such a remark with downright cynicism. She had a good figure, but her fair complexion was a curse and she was all too aware of the freckles that sprinkled her skin. Nevertheless, she didn't think it altogether unnatural for Justin St John to feel a fleeting impulse to kiss her.

The situation had been fraught with a lot of feelings, and things had got slightly out of hand. That was all. It wouldn't happen again. After he had had time to think about it, Justin St John would realise that. He was a mature adult with too much experience to let such a little incident upset him unduly. And she would soon show him that she could be completely professional. She would ring him and offer her services again. It was the least she could do after what *he* had done.

However, when Kelly reached her office she had second thoughts on the matter. Perhaps it was too soon after last night for Justin St John to change his mind. If she telephoned and he refused again, it might cement his decision. And she didn't want that. On the other hand, if the pain was bad enough, and she left it a day or two, he might be in a more persuadable frame of mind when she rang.

That was the better course, Kelly decided. She couldn't risk another outright rejection from him.

There was still the matter of the horses to be resolved. However, she was now hopeful that Justin St John would be reasonable once she had a chance to explain everything to him. All she had to do was time her approach correctly.

The day passed. Kelly could not help comparing her male patients to Justin St John. Not one of them had a body to match his, although many were younger. A couple of them tried to flirt with her, but she found their attentions callow and irritating. It was a relief to go home.

Her grandfather unconsciously echoed her own thoughts over dinner that night. 'Is he the kind of man to change his mind, Kelly?'

'I wouldn't think so, Grandpa,' she answered. But he might if she waited long enough, she hoped privately. And if he was thinking the same kind of thoughts she was thinking...

'The judge might be right,' her grandfather remarked doubtfully. 'Justin St John could have been fobbing you off while he...'

'No!' Kelly said with absolute conviction. She fixed her grandfather with steady green eyes. 'I'm certain he was sincere. We've got nothing to worry about, Grandpa.'

He heaved a sigh of satisfaction, but after a few moments a frown descended. 'What about the horses? Is he going to let you ride them?'

'Uh... I didn't have the opportunity to ask. It didn't seem to be... quite the right moment,' she excused.

'Hmm...' Her grandfather ruminated on that for several minutes. 'Haven't you got them entered for Dapto?'

'Yes. But I thought I'd wait a day or two, Grandpa. After all, we've just won a big concession from him. I didn't want to press my luck. And if he rings up for physiotherapy again...'

Her grandfather's face suddenly split into a wide grin. 'You reckon if it worked once it could work twice. Justin St John might be slippery like the judge says. But that's one way of pinning him down, eh, Kelly?'

He laughed, his good humour restored, and Kelly laughed with him, pretending that was precisely the plan, although she was considerably less confident about it than she had been this morning.

The more she thought about it, the more uncertain she became that Justin St John would change his mind about seeing her again. He was not the kind of man who liked to acknowledge any weakness, not even pain. And she kept remembering the flash of revulsion on his face. It nagged at her mind. What was so wrong about her that he should feel so revolted by the temptation to kiss her?

No call came from Marian Park requesting her services. Kelly fretted through three days, then decided she had to take the initiative before it was too late to break the impasse.

Roy Farley answered her call.

'Thank you for your concern, Miss Hanrahan,' he said politely, 'but Mr St John does not require any more physiotherapy.'

Which had to be a lie, Kelly reasoned. 'May I speak to him, Mr Farley? He may not realise...'

'I'm sorry, Miss Hanrahan,' he cut in decisively. 'Mr St John is not available. I'll tell him you called, if that is what you want. Should he wish to get back to you, I'm sure he will.'

'Yes. Thank you,' Kelly said, completely squashed. No comeback possible on that line!

Well, let him suffer, if that was how he felt, Kelly thought belligerently. But that didn't solve the problem of the horses. And the Dapto show-jumping events were fast approaching. The horses needed to be worked. How was she going to get to Justin St John if he insisted on being unavailable? She didn't want to antagonise the man. Certainly not while Grandpa's land rights were still being settled.

It was a very tricky situation. She couldn't delay much longer. Already it was too late to get the horses into peak readiness. Rasputin was probably her only chance. The big black stallion—all sixteen point three hands of him—was a born jumper. If Justin St John would only take the time to listen to her...but how to make him?

The solution came two days later.

Kelly came home from work to a jubilant grand-father. 'The title deeds!' he shouted to her from the veranda, waving a sheaf of papers in the air. 'Delivered by special courier. They came this afternoon. He really did it, Kelly! We've got them!'

He rushed her inside to the kitchen and laid the important papers out on the table. 'All signed up and legal!' he gloated happily. 'I got Tom Kennedy to come and check them over. I could hardly believe it, but it's true all right. Tom says they're the real McCoy. No doubt about it. Judge Moffat was wrong.'

'I told you that Justin St John meant it, Grandpa,' Kelly reminded him, although even she felt dazed at the speed with which the promise had been fulfilled.

It was so good of him to have done it so fast! For one thing, it showed his power. For another, his integrity. And also the kindest consideration.

Kelly made her decision immediately. He should be thanked. Straight away. In person. It was the only decent thing to do.

She heaved a sigh of relief as the idea blossomed inside her. It was certainly the right course of action. And what better way to reach a friendly understanding with him? She was truly grateful for what he'd done, and she could show her gratitude. She wouldn't offer him physiotherapy again. She would insist he have it. And whenever he needed relief from pain, she would come to Marian Park and not charge him any extra for it.

And if he was as nice as he had been over settling Grandpa's land rights, and let her ride his horses, she wouldn't charge him any fee at all.

'We ought to thank him, Grandpa. You stay here and have your supper. I'll go on up to Marian Park and do it right now,' she announced decisively.

Her grandfather lifted a startled look. He was still reaching for words when Kelly swung into action. She didn't want to discuss the point. This was her best excuse to get Justin St John to see her, and she wasn't going to let anything or anyone stop her from speaking to him.

She whirled out of the kitchen, ran down the veranda steps to her car, leapt in, gunned the motor and drove up to Marian Park with absolute determination in her heart.

CHAPTER FIVE

KELLY couldn't remember ever having knocked on Henry Lloyd's front door before. She had always walked right in, never doubting for a moment that she would be welcomed. It felt strange, discomfiting, having to wait for admittance. Worse to think she might not be admitted at all. But Kelly was not about to let that happen.

She was all primed up to tackle any argument. When the door opened, it was a pleasant relief to see Mrs Ryan's familiar face. The housekeeper had been at Marian Park for the last ten years and was an old friend. She was a plump, cheerful soul, past middle age but wearing very well, and many a time Kelly had been hugged to her generous bosom.

'Kelly!' Her smile was a beam of pleasure. 'I heard the good news from Tom Kennedy's wife, and I'm so happy for you,' she added in a conspiratorial whisper.

No doubt the Crooked Creek grapevine was working overtime, Kelly thought, but it made things easier for her. 'Thanks, Mrs Ryan. And I've come to thank Mr St John in person. Is he in?'

Her face fell. 'No. He's not.' A struggle of loyalties clearly overwhelmed the good-natured woman. 'That's the official line. But in actual fact he is here, Kelly,' she hissed. 'All I can do for you is take you into the drawing-room, and then tell Mr Farley you asked to see him. But you'll have to talk your way past him. I don't dare...'

'That'll be fine, Mrs Ryan,' Kelly assured her gratefully. 'And thanks a million.'

'It's not like what it was, Kelly,' the housekeeper said mournfully. 'But at least we all still have our jobs here. That's better than it could have been.'

Kelly pressed her arm in silent sympathy as she accompanied her inside. 'I don't think Mr St John can be a bad sort, Mrs Ryan. Not totally bad,' she assured her in a discreet whisper.

The housekeeper shook her head, obviously in two minds about that. 'He seems a kind enough man, Kelly,' she murmured. 'But everyone's so upset about this thing with the sheep. And he shouldn't have stopped you from riding...'

'Maybe he'll change his mind.'

The memory of Henry Lloyd's benevolent reign at Marian Park saddened them both as they entered the drawing-room. Nothing had been changed here, yet they knew everything had changed.

'I wish you luck, my dear,' Mrs Ryan sighed, and patted Kelly's hand before leaving to fetch Roy Farley.

Kelly's gaze automatically lifted to Noni's portrait above the fireplace, and she drew strength from it. Noni had died riding, but she would never have given it up if she had lived. And neither would Kelly give it up! Henry Lloyd had been proud of her for following in Noni's footsteps, and she would continue to do so. Justin St John had to understand that.

'Miss Hanrahan...'

She swung around to face Roy Farley, who remained poised in the doorway, his face carved in polite reserve.

'You wanted to see me about something?' he enquired.

'Where's Mr St John?' she demanded to know.

'I'm here to handle Mr St John's business.'

'Not the kind of business I want to talk about, Mr Farley. It's personal.'

'I'm sorry, Miss Hanrahan, but...'

'I'm not budging from this house until I see Mr St John. You can tell him that from me, Mr Farley,' she declared, striking a determined stand.

He stiffened into aloof dignity. 'Miss Hanrahan...'

'Please go and tell him!' Kelly commanded, her voice lifting to a loud ringing tone. 'It's ridiculous for him to be hiding behind you. And if he can't stand on his own two feet, then you'd better lead me to him. For one thing, he needs more physiotherapy. And it's ridiculous to deny that, too.'

'Mr St John has no further business with you, Miss Hanrahan,' he said frostily. 'If you can't accept that, I'm sorry. But if you won't leave of your own accord, I'll pick you up myself and carry you outside.'

'Lay one finger on me and I'll have the law on to you,' Kelly threatened fiercely.

'You're trespassing, Miss Hanrahan.'

'I'm being friendly, for heaven's sake!' Kelly cried in furious frustration. 'This situation is crazy! Who does Justin St John think he is, anyway? Another Howard Hughes?'

Roy Farley started walking towards her, his rugged face grim with purpose.

'Don't do it!' Kelly warned. 'Marian Park isn't the city, you know. And neither is Crooked Creek. You can't treat people here like unwanted rubbish...'

'Roy, I'll handle this!'

Justin St John's voice cracked across the room and spun Kelly around. Roy Farley had used the foyer entrance. Justin St John stood at the double doors which opened into the music-room, emanating an authority that denied he hid behind anything.

He wore grey trousers and a grey and white striped shirt with crisp white collar and cuffs. His black hair was neatly groomed but his face was more harshly drawn than Kelly had ever seen it. The grey eyes bored into her with steely disdain, making Kelly intensely aware that she had not stopped to tidy her appearance before racing up to see him.

Her hair was thick enough and heavy enough to hang smoothly to her shoulders, even though it hadn't been brushed for hours, but she probably didn't have a scrap of make-up left on her face. Her freckles would be showing and her lipstick worn off. The fabric of her dark green dress was a polyester mix, so it shouldn't be crumpled, but the shirt-dress style was more practical than elegant, and she felt very ordinary and unattractive.

Justin St John's gaze flicked past her. Roy Farley hesitated. He was given a nod of dismissal, and the secretary left.

Justin St John returned his attention to Kelly. 'My physical and mental well-being is my own concern, Miss Hanrahan. Not yours,' he said pointedly. 'You now have your own part of Marian Park. I have mine. If I choose to seclude myself here, that's my business. You have no right to thrust your... unwanted presence on me or my property. Do I make myself clear?'

'No!' Kelly burst out indignantly. 'No, you don't! And I won't accept it, either. The other night you turned into a human being and I don't see why you can't stay that way. I came up here to thank you, as any well-mannered person would, and I will not be treated like a... like a pariah! Why should I?'

His face tightened. 'I told you I didn't need to be thanked.'

'Well, you're going to be thanked whether you like it or not!' Kelly retorted. Her hands flew out to emphasise her points. 'You could have tied Grandpa up in the law courts for years, but you didn't. You were kind and generous and...and big-hearted to push everything through so fast. Not many people would have cared about an old man's feelings. It was very good of you. And that's why I'm here. I want to thank you!'

His face relaxed its hard reserve during her passionate recital and his mouth actually curled into an ironic little smile. 'Consider me thanked. Now, if that is all, Miss Hanrahan...'

'No, it's not all! In fact, I've hardly begun!' Her eyes flashed down to the walking-stick he was leaning on, then up again to challenge him. 'That leg is still giving you pain, isn't it? And don't say it's not my business. You called me in as a physiotherapist and...'

'And I paid you off,' he cut in with smooth and deadly precision. 'That is my prerogative, Miss Hanrahan.' A ghost of a smile twitched across his face. 'I didn't like the way you...er...wanted to tear into me.'

'Oh!' Kelly stamped her foot and turned away from him in disgust. She paced the floor in angry agitation, throwing him accusing looks. 'That was before. And you know it. And I didn't do it even when I had most reason to. You're being utterly unreasonable. You know you need treatment. What's wrong with me giving it to you?'

His expression tightened up again. 'No fault lies with you,' he stated flatly. 'The choice was...is...mine.'

She flapped her hands in helpless appeal against his intransigence. 'It makes no sense to refuse what I can do for you.'

'It does to me,' he grated.

She didn't know why she kept beating her head against what was obviously a brick wall, but a compelling urge to reach him drove her feet forward. 'Please... let me help you,' she implored softly.

His whole body tensed at her approach. 'Why?' he barked at her.

Kelly faltered to a standstill a few paces short of him, sensing a resistance so deep that it seemed foolhardy to go on. She actually felt a prickle of danger at the back of her neck. But she ignored the warning signals.

'Because I want to,' she said with direct simplicity. 'And I don't believe you like suffering pain.'

'No.' His eyes burned at her with a brief, turbulent glitter. 'No!' he repeated with more vehemence, then wrenched his gaze from hers, lifting it beyond her, fixing it with seemingly anguished obsession on the portrait of Noni.

Kelly was left hanging in a vacuum, shut out by him but with nowhere to go. Positive action was the only answer her bewildered mind threw up, and she stepped forward and touched his arm in an attempt to force his attention back to her.

'Why won't you let me help you?'

His eyes stabbed down with glittering savagery. 'Because you're a child! A child who has cost me too much already!'

His voice was shocking in its harsh brutality. There was almost hatred in his tone. Certainly bitterness...of a cup that had filled to the brim and overflowed.

She stared up at him, transfixed by something she didn't understand. Intuitively she was aware that he knew something she didn't...and the knowledge was an old, old agony that washed through him as he stared blindly into her eyes, not seeing the woman she was, but something or someone else. And her heart twisted with an unfamiliar fear.

He was virtually a stranger. How could he know something about her that she didn't know? Why did she feel tied to him by something she didn't understand? Yet the feeling was there, binding them together. And when he lifted his hand and touched her face...it did not feel like the hand of a stranger.

A muscle in his jaw contracted. He removed his hand from her cheek and clenched it into a fist before slowly dropping it to his side. The tight, shuttered look came back to his face, closing in all vestige of emotion, and he turned away from her, leaning heavily on his walking-stick as he made his way to the closest armchair. He clutched the back-rest as if he needed extra support.

'Would you please leave? I don't wish to be unkind, but I really don't want you here, Kelly,' he said quietly, his voice very flat and controlled.

'Somehow I frighten you, don't I?' she blurted out, speaking from instinct rather than any reason she could think of.

'Yes, you frighten me.' He laughed harshly, and his voice broke into bitter mockery, mouthing words that lashed himself more than her. 'You frighten me very much. Think...if you wish...that I'm running away from you. It's close enough to the truth. The further you are from me, the better. So go away. Go home. Leave me to my own devices.'

'I've never run from anything in my life,' Kelly said stubbornly. 'And I'm not starting now.'

'Well...' He rolled the word out grimly as he turned back to her, and the barely controlled ferocity of his expression made Kelly's heart flutter with apprehension. '...let's see if this doesn't frighten you as much as it does me.'

He tossed his walking-stick aside as if it was no longer of any account. He took her wrist and pulled her into an embrace that crushed her body against his. Kelly was so stunned by the unexpected action that his fingers had thrust through her hair and dragged her head back before she could catch her breath, let alone begin to protest or even think to resist his formidable strength.

As he bent his head purposefully towards hers, the look of startled vulnerability in her eyes gave Justin St John a moment's anguished pause, and he cursed himself for a fool. He had wanted to kiss her roughly, hurt and intimidate her, so that she would cease this mad confrontation and leave him alone in his world of pain. Give to her some of what she had made him feel.

But she was innocent of any wrong to him. It had been his choice. *His!* She didn't know—couldn't know—what hell she wrought, simply with her presence. She had been too young. She would always be too young. Her lips were quivering.

Just this once. Just this once, he promised himself. I'll give in to the temptation to kiss her just this once, and I swear I'll never touch her again. I'll send her away and make sure she stays away. But just this once...

Kelly's heart was thumping chaotically. She was barely aware of his hold on her gentling. He was going to kiss her. She felt his lips seal lightly against her own. Surprise and relief swept away the fear that had gripped her stomach. It wasn't a hostile kiss. For some inexplicable reason his intention had changed, and Kelly sensed she had won a major victory.

A warm pleasure rippled through her. The beguiling sensuality of his lips brushing over hers, the tantalising changes of pressure, the heightened awareness of the feel of his body against hers—Kelly surrendered without a moment's thought to what he was doing to her, and felt a heady glow of something wonderful, super-charged, an infinity of dazzling possibilities.

He stirred slightly, as if to pull away. She felt the hardening of his body, knew she was exciting him, and revelled in it. She moved one of her hands up to curl around his head and hold him still so she could keep savouring the tingling sensuality of his kiss. But it changed with her willing encouragement, grew more demanding with her eager response, passionate, hungry for all she would give him.

She pressed closer, excitingly aware of the growing sensitivity in her breasts as they softened against the unyielding wall of his chest. His arms tightened around her, pulling her even closer. She felt every muscle in his body tighten in need, and was deliciously relaxed herself, giving, melting into him.

In sheer wanton bliss she opened her mouth to his, and exulted in the wildly erotic invasion of his tongue, her senses aflame with a desire she had never experienced before, a need for more and more sensation, intimacy, knowledge, power...all of him!

His mouth wrenched away from hers with shocking abruptness. A guttural expression of repugnance was expelled on a long, ragged breath. He grasped her upper arms and pushed her from him, forcibly holding her away from any contact with his body. And, while she was still dazed and quivering from the needs that he had aroused, he shocked her even further with the cold, deliberate savagery of a verbal rejection.

'That's where it ends! You've been taught a lesson. Now go home, little girl. You're out of your depth with me. And always will be.'

He moved back to arm's length before he finally released her, and the look on his face was that of a condemned man who was seeing the world for the last time.

As shaken as she was, Kelly defiantly stood her ground. No way was she going to turn tail and run at his command! Nor was he going to frighten her with his assumed violence, or browbeat her in any way. He could not deny what had just passed between them. And it had been the same for him as it had for her. She knew it!

A film of tears lent a piercing brilliance to her green eyes, stabbing him with wounded but unremitting pride. 'I've just proved I'm not a little girl. And I'm not a child. If you can't handle the fact that I'm a woman, that's OK with me. But let's not get the insults the wrong way around. Are you man enough for me?'

She paused, taking the time to place her hands aggressively on her hips, stubbornly striking a pose that denied the churning distress that was making jelly of her insides. She could feel her lips trembling and bit them, fighting for more composure before she continued.

'Why do you have to run away from me?' she taunted.

His grimace was all bitter irony.

'Let me make you whole again. Let me help you to walk properly,' she shot at him, desperately seeking to get under his skin. 'I'm not interested in your self-pity! It's the person inside that's important!'

A bleak weariness dragged over Justin St John's face. He was as unshiftable as granite. 'No more, Kelly. Please go. I trust you don't need me to show you to the door,' he said with tired finality.

Kelly's chin lifted in determined defiance. 'There is one last piece of unfinished business left between us.'

The weariness cracked back into ferocity. 'What, for pete's sake? What more can there be between us?' He seemed at the end of his tether and he glowered at her with furious impatience.

The situation couldn't have been worse, Kelly thought despairingly. But he left her no option. This was the bottom line. No loopholes for bargaining. No room to manoeuvre. Not the slightest chance of any softening-up process, or sliding amicably into the subject.

She heaved a resigned sigh and spelled it out. 'The horses that you stopped me from riding are more mine than yours. I can't deny that Henry Lloyd bought them, but he bought them especially for me. I chose them, and worked them, and trained . . .'

'It was you? You taking the black stallion over the jumps?' His voice sounded half strangled, and all colour drained from his face, leaving it stark with shock.

Kelly hesitated, uncertain what his reaction meant and hopelessly unsettled by it. 'If you saw anyone riding Rasputin over the practice jumps, it would have been me,' she replied tentatively. 'He doesn't respond to anyone else. But that was before you cut me off from having any more to do with the horses. And that was totally unfair. I tried to see you, to talk to you. But then you were trying to get Grandpa off his land and we had to fight that first...'

Justin St John's eyes had closed tight and he was shaking his head as though punch-drunk. 'No,' he groaned. 'I can't... I won't...'

'If you'll please just listen to me...' Kelly begged.

'No!'

The harsh negative rattled in her ears, but Kelly couldn't accept it. 'I promise you I won't get in your way. You won't even see me if you don't want to. I'll take——'

'No! Never!' he yelled at her, angry colour rushing back into his face. His eyes were glazed, fixed with maniacal determination.

'It's not fair on me. Or the horses,' she cried frantically. 'You can't keep them penned up in the stables. They need...'

He banged his hands together in violent rejection. 'They can rot there forever for all I care. If I don't shoot them first!'

The venomous hatred in his voice was like a fist-blow to Kelly's heart. 'You couldn't!' she gasped. 'You wouldn't do that! Those horses are beautiful...truly beautiful!'

Her stricken look seemed to touch him. He appeared totally distracted for a moment. Then he jerked his body into action and started limping towards the doors that led into the foyer.

'Go home, Kelly Hanrahan!' he ordered harshly, and the back that was turned to her was rigid and unyielding. 'There is nothing you can say—no words, no sentiments, no pleading that you can think of—that can persuade me to change my mind. As long as those horses are in my keeping, you will never ride them again!'

Desperation drove Kelly after him. She grabbed his arm, halting his progress. He tried to tear it out of her grasp, but she clung on, forcing him to listen to her. 'You can't mean that!' she begged. 'I've been jumping them for years. It's my life...'

'It was Noni Lloyd's death!' he retorted, his eyes blazing at her in wild, impassioned accusation. 'Doesn't that mean anything to you?'

'It was an accident!' Kelly blazed back at him. 'If Noni had been given a second chance, she would have gone on and...'

He grabbed her upper arms and shook her. 'There was no second chance for Noni! You have your life! Be content with that,' he hissed at her through clenched teeth. 'And there's more to life than show-jumping!'

Tears welled into Kelly's eyes and she was helpless to stop them from trickling down her cheeks. 'It's all I want to do,' she sobbed. 'All I ever wanted...'

'Kelly, I'm sorry.' It was an anguished sigh, and without another word he gathered her into a gentle embrace and softly pressed her head on to his shoulder.

Kelly's heart raced with exultant triumph. He was going to give in. He really liked her. And wanted her. She would talk him around to a sympathetic understanding. They could be together. Learn everything about each other.

She savoured the wonderful thoughts as he rubbed his cheek across her hair and relished the warmth and strength of him as he heaved another deep sigh.

'I'm sorry,' he repeated heavily. 'But I can't let you have it, Kelly. Anything, but not that. Not that! If I have to destroy the horses to keep you from them, I will.'

The sense of betrayal was so sharp, so hurtful, that she whirled away from him and lashed out with all the pulsating torment of her lacerated feelings. 'The trouble with you, Mr Justin St John, is that you've had your own way for far too long! You don't know what it's like to have to struggle in order to succeed.' She shook her fist at him, so overwrought that she barely knew what she was doing or saying. 'Well, I do! And I've worked hard at it. And I'm not going to let you take it away from me.'

'Kelly, please...'

She saw his strained face through a blur as the idea formed, took hold. However reckless it was didn't matter. 'You've had your say. Now I'm having mine! If you're going to shoot Rasputin, then you're going to have to shoot me as well. I'm taking him away from you.'

And, before he could reach out a hand to stop her, she turned and ran.

'Kelly, please——' He lunged after her but she was too quick for him. 'Stop, Kelly! Come back...'

The front door was opened and slammed shut, punctuating her headstrong defiance.

Justin tried to ignore the pain in his leg, but he knew he couldn't make it to the stables without the support of the walking-stick. He almost fell in his haste to scoop it up from the floor. Cursing with the frustration of his disability, he made it to the front door as fast as he could and hobbled down the steps to the driveway.

She had abandoned her car. He just caught a glimpse of her running figure before she disappeared behind the hedge that lined the right-hand fork of the driveway. Justin had no doubt about her destination. It didn't occur to him to call out for assistance. He wouldn't allow any other man to *touch* her. Kelly was his responsibility.

That big black rogue of a horse was just like the one Noni had ridden to her death. How Henry Lloyd had ever allowed Kelly to have him, Justin couldn't comprehend. Blind indulgence! Madness! He had to stop her.

He should have sold the damned stallion the moment he had started giving the stable-hand trouble. Then Kelly could never have got near him again.

But he hadn't known it was her!

His hip was on fire with agony, but he pushed himself on, frantic to prevent the child . . . no, the girl—the woman . . . from endangering her life with such foolhardy recklessness. He couldn't let her do it to herself!

She had left the gate to the stable-yard open.

Justin quickened his pace, uncaring of what damage he was doing to his leg. A sense of triumph gripped him as he clutched the top railing, dragged the gate shut, and shot the bolt home.

He heard the clatter of hooves on the cement floor of the stable-block, but Kelly was too late now. He leaned against the gate, exhausted, but able to relax, knowing she couldn't go on with this madness.

Pain swamped over him. But that didn't matter. He had stopped her. She couldn't get out of the yard.

He heaved himself around to face her, and experienced another wave of shock. She sat on the big black stallion bareback. No saddle. No stirrups for control. Only a halter and the thin strap of reins to hold a horse that measured nearly seventeen hands. The huge, lethal power of the animal was heart-joltingly evident as it pranced with excitable impatience. Sheer horror drained the blood from Justin's face.

Kelly called out to him before he could recover himself. 'You shouldn't have followed me. That hip is going to need working on. Come and see me tomorrow.'

'Get off that horse!' he shouted with all the force he could gather. 'Be sensible, Kelly! You can't get away now.'

'Tomorrow. In my office,' she yelled back.

The horse reared slightly as she gathered in the reins. Justin couldn't bring himself to believe she'd do it. But she was setting the horse for the jump.

'No!' he screamed at her. 'Kelly, no!'

But the black stallion was already in stride, heading straight for the gate, picking up speed, urged on by a woman who had lost touch with all reality. She wasn't even wearing a riding-helmet!

Justin's heart was in his mouth as the horse lifted, but the mighty stallion cleared the gate with space to spare. He landed smoothly, and without the slightest hesitation in his stride raced on down the road, imbued with the heady spirit of freedom.

Its bareback rider never looked back, never shifted in her seat.

However grudging the feeling was, Justin couldn't help but admire the way Kelly Hanrahan could ride.

CHAPTER SIX

KELLY worried about Justin St John as she galloped off on Rasputin. His face had looked so white and strained. But she did not slacken the great stallion's pace. She had to get the horse away and safe as quickly as she could. She didn't draw rein until she was over the knoll and out of sight.

'Now for cross-country, Rasputin,' she said, and patted his shoulder encouragingly before wheeling him to face the fence. The small time advantage she had before Justin St John could organise a pursuit had to be optimised. The only way of ensuring she would not be caught was to get off the road and stay off it.

'This will be something of an endurance test, my beauty,' she crooned to the horse, whose ears pricked appreciatively. 'But you can do it, can't you?'

Rasputin whinnied eager agreement. He responded instantly to Kelly's urging and leapt the fence with arrogant ease. He almost bolted across the sheep pasture, eager to take the next jump, and however many more Kelly wanted him to take.

Kelly only kept a light control on him. She didn't try to temper his exuberance until she was sure they could not be spotted by anyone giving chase. 'Easy boy!' she called, and reined him in to a relaxed canter. 'It's a long way to the judge's place,' she explained to him, 'and I don't want you breaking a leg in a rabbit-hole.'

Rasputin gave a contemptuous snort, but he was happy to follow her lead.

Kelly figured that Judge Moffat would be sympathetic to her cause. He was a horse lover himself. And it could only help that he was extremely put out with Justin St John about the sheep business. Rasputin would be safe at the Moffats' place.

After all, who would ever think of looking in the judge's stables for a stolen horse? Even if they did, the judge would never grant a search warrant against himself. No place could be safer until she could think how else to deal with the problem.

Having settled that in her mind, Kelly's thoughts automatically drifted back to Justin St John. It distressed her that he might have hurt his leg chasing after her, and trying to prevent her from leaving the stable-yard. He should have called for Roy Farley. Or someone else.

However, she felt no guilt whatsoever about taking Rasputin. That Justin St John had threatened to destroy him... Kelly shuddered at the thought of such a rash and terrible criminal act.

Of course, people did occasionally have an accident on horses, but in all her years Kelly had never had the slightest injury. What had happened to Noni was a freak accident. Kelly was not going to stop show-jumping because Justin St John was opposed to it!

But she wished he could be reasonable. She didn't want to be enemies with him. She wanted...but it was no use thinking about that now. He had no right to separate her from her horses!

The sun had set by the time Kelly reached Judge Moffat's stud-farm. She walked Rasputin up the driveway, not wanting to alarm anyone with their arrival. She could see the judge and his wife sitting on the homestead veranda, enjoying the balmy twilight before going inside for the night. It was a favourite time of day for most people on the land.

Arlene Moffat saw her first and rose from her chair in surprised curiosity. 'Why, it's Kelly! On Rasputin!' Her voice carried on the still evening air, but she raised it in sheer pleasure. 'Hello, there! You're riding again.'

'Yes, Mrs Moffat,' Kelly called back. She cantered up the last stretch and slid off Rasputin as the judge rose and came to the veranda railing to join his wife. Kelly made her appeal directly to him. 'I need your advice, Judge. I had to take Rasputin away from Marian Park. Justin St John was threatening to shoot him rather than let me ride him. I didn't have Justin St John's permission. He...er...tried to stop me. But I couldn't leave Rasputin with him after he said that. I had to...'

'How could he be so dreadful?' Arlene Moffat cried in sympathetic protest. 'You did right, Kelly! Henry Lloyd meant those horses to be for you...'

'And possession is nine tenths of the law!' the judge quoted with relish. 'Good for you, Kelly. I reckon this might teach Justin St John a lesson about doing things right. In fact, he needs every lesson he can get!'

'I was wondering if I could stable Rasputin with your horses, Judge? Just for a while...' Kelly pleaded.

'Certainly. Certainly,' he rolled out with gusto.

'As long as you like, Kelly,' Arlene put in determinedly. 'And you can use our horse-float to get to the show-jumping. We'll stand by you. And so will all of Crooked Creek. I'll see to that.'

The power of holding office on all of the local committees rang in Arlene Moffat's voice, and Kelly knew her support was no small thing. When it came to arousing public opinion, Arlene Moffat could teach professional lobbyists a thing or two.

'That's more than kind,' Kelly said with heartfelt gratitude.

'Only right.' She turned to her husband. 'Now, you go and help Kelly stable Rasputin, Ezra, and then run her home in the car. She looks worn out.'

Kelly felt more battered emotionally than physically, but she did not dispute the point. However, her legal—or illegal—position still fretted her mind, and while she and the judge were getting Rasputin safely stowed away in the stables Kelly broached the subject again.

'Don't fret yourself, Kelly. It won't come to anything. But even if it did, no jury in Crooked Creek would convict you of horse-stealing,' he assured her. 'There is a rough precedent. They didn't do it to Harry Redmond in Roma, and they won't do it to you.'

'Who was Harry Redmond?' Kelly asked, not regretting her action, but unable to completely squash her apprehension as to its outcome.

The judge chuckled. 'He took a few thousand head of cattle and drove them down the Birdsville Track to South Australia where he sold them. Finally he was caught and hauled back to Roma to stand trial for stealing them. The evidence was watertight. But every man Jack on the jury admired Harry Redmond. They wished they'd had the guts to do it themselves. The jury was unanimous. They didn't even leave the room to discuss it. Acquitted him without a qualm.' The judge winked at Kelly with conspiratorial pleasure. 'Same will apply to you. People will admire what you've done.' His florid face broke into a wide grin. 'They never did hold another trial for cattle-stealing in Roma.'

'Well, I hope it doesn't come to that,' Kelly sighed. 'If Justin St John would only see reason...'

'Reason or not, that horse is yours to ride, Kelly. And don't you worry. We'll fix it, one way or another. Justin St John is not getting away with this iniquity.'

Somewhat cheered by the Moffats' support, Kelly tried to relax on the drive home, but the thought of what might be waiting for her there was a strain on her nerves. She asked the judge to drop her at the turn-off to Marian Park, not wanting to get him any more involved than he already was. Besides, if he was seen with her, a connection might be made to Rasputin's whereabouts.

Kelly had forgotten all about abandoning her car at Marian Park until she saw it parked just inside the gateway to her grandfather's property. So someone had returned it. And what did that mean? Were they waiting for her at home? What would Justin St John do?

Apprehension knotted her stomach, but defiance put some stiffening into her resolve not to back down, whatever happened. The car-key was hanging in the ignition where she had left it. Kelly boldly drove the Toyota up to the house. There was no point in sneaking around anyway. Rasputin was safe, and whatever the consequences of her actions she would face them with her chin held high.

To her relief and astonishment, Kelly found her grandfather alone in the house. He knew nothing of what had happened. In fact, he thought she was just returning from Marian Park and was rather peeved that she had been gone so long. No one had been asking after her, either in person or by telephone.

It took some time to relate the whole sequence of events, and her grandfather listened with interest and awe and pride. Finally he declared that Kelly couldn't have done anything else under the circumstances, and Judge Moffat's advice was absolutely right. In fact, he might even let the judge win their next chess game. He was too good a man to be subjected to too many losses.

As for Justin St John, he was a very confusing person. 'Can't make him out at all...giving with the one hand and taking with the other.' Michael O'Reilly shook his head in puzzlement. 'But one thing's certain, Kelly. He hasn't made any charge of horse-stealing at the police station. Sergeant Connelly would have let me know if you were in any trouble there.'

They ruminated over that undoubtable truth for several minutes.

'Maybe he's seen the light and changed his mind. Just as he did with my land,' her grandfather suggested.

Kelly sighed. 'I don't think so, Grandpa.' She remembered Justin St John's words all too vividly. For him to change his mind about show-jumping seemed beyond the realms of possibility. 'But miracles do happen,' she added out loud.

And her grandfather was certainly right about Justin St John being a very confusing person. Kelly had edited the kissing part out of her story, but she thought about it a lot when she went to bed that night.

There was no denying that she felt very attracted to the man, despite the age difference between them. In fact, she had never felt any of the things he made her feel. It wasn't just a sexual thing, like that stupid infatuation she had had at college. She didn't know...didn't understand what it was. Except that it was disturbingly strong.

To say she had fallen in love with Justin St John was obviously premature. She had only met him twice. But the impact both times had certainly imprinted him on her mind. And her heart was not behaving normally at all.

Perhaps it was only because he had struck at issues that meant so much to her...such as Grandpa's land and the show-jumping. Her emotions had been well and truly stirred, and his reaction to her had stirred them even further. Perhaps that was it.

All the same, she wouldn't mind him kissing her again. Although that was highly improbable, considering the present conflict between them.

Yet...why hadn't he done something about her taking Rasputin? Why had he let her get away with it? Or was he simply waiting until tomorrow, to see if she returned the prize stallion?

Undoubtedly that had to be what he was expecting!

Well, he'd be waiting a long time, Kelly vowed.

Kelly drove off to work particularly early the next morning. If there was going to be trouble with Justin St John, she didn't want her grandfather in the middle of it, getting over-excited and upset. He had only just recovered from the last lot of stress. She would handle this by herself...if that was possible.

As soon as she reached her office she telephoned the Moffats, reporting that nothing had happened to her as yet, and learning that Rasputin was in fine fettle and quite at home in his new stall. Kelly promised to keep Arlene abreast of any pertinent news and rang off.

So far, so good, she thought, but her nerves were definitely in a bad way. Although Kelly called her place of business an office it actually comprised four rooms—three for treating her patients and a small waiting-room with a reception desk. She fidgeted through all of them—tidying, dusting, straightening the pile of magazines—keeping herself busy while she waited for the first appointment at nine o'clock.

It was a relief to hear the front door opening just five minutes short of the hour. Kelly hurried into the waiting-room to greet her expected patient. She stopped dead when she saw who it was.

He leaned heavily on his walking-stick as he shut the door behind him. The grey eyes regarded Kelly with steely intensity. His face gave nothing away, not even the slightest flicker of the pain he had to be suffering with his leg.

The click of the door activated Kelly's defence mechanisms. Her mind shrieked that she would not be intimidated. She had right on her side. She would not back down from the action she had taken. Never. No matter what he threatened. But none of these brave resolutions seemed to work.

'You came?' The trite words trickled out of her mouth before she could stop them.

As much as Kelly would have liked to believe that Justin St John had ventured into her office for physiotherapy, it was hardly within the realms of possibility. It had to be over the horses. He was too determined on having his own way to let her get away with stealing Rasputin, particularly when he had gone through so much physical pain to stop her.

'I wanted to see you,' he said grimly, his lips barely moving.

Kelly remembered all too clearly how those lips felt moving over her own. They had certainly done some moving then. She felt the heat rising in her body. It was difficult to block out all the other things she had felt in his embrace, especially when he was standing right in front of her.

Kelly tried to wrench her mind on to something else. She didn't want to think about what Justin St John was doing to her. Under the circumstances, she didn't want to discuss the subject of horses and show-jumping with him either.

Which only left work. And whether he wanted it or not, Justin St John did need physiotherapy. And she had told him to come to her office for it.

'I'm glad you took my advice,' she said brightly. 'I've been waiting for you. I can fit you in straight away.'

Whatever he was expecting, it wasn't that. He could not conceal his surprise. It flashed across his face for an instant before he could control it. Then the muscles of his face tightened, and all expression was carefully blanked from his face.

His eyes narrowed as he stared at her assessingly. It was as if he was seeing her for the first time. Kelly didn't give him time to think about it. For some incomprehensible reason, she felt she held a momentary advantage over him. But it was one which could be quickly lost. It was necessary to act immediately.

She strode across the room to draw aside the curtain which lent privacy to one of the treatment cubicles. She motioned Justin St John forward. 'If you'll just come through here, and...er...get prepared...'

It had been on the tip of her tongue to ask him to take his trousers off—which was what she meant—but just the imagery and possible implications of the words sent another tide of heat washing right through her body. She quickly swung on her heel to lead the way for him. She hoped the hot flush would recede as fast as it had embarrassed her.

'You obviously got home safely!' The words were drawled in a low tone of voice and were sarcastic.

Kelly wheeled around. Justin St John had only followed her as far as the curtained doorway, and was propped against the frame, his eyes following her every movement.

'Yes,' Kelly said defensively. 'I know the country around here very well. I didn't have any trouble.'

'As yet,' he breathed.

Another knock on her door had her racing from the room, almost bumping into him. 'That's another of my patients,' she murmured, side-stepping past him in anxious haste, too shatteringly aware of him to meet his eyes. 'Please go ahead and get ready, and I'll be with you as soon as possible. Today I want to start with some tests.'

He didn't say a word, and Kelly didn't glance back at him. She hoped quite desperately that he was doing what she'd told him, but nothing was certain with Justin St John. She hadn't anticipated him turning up at her office.

In her mind she was already readjusting her appointment book, working out how she would cope with one extra patient. Others would have to wait a little longer and have a little bit less treatment than normal. She would make it up to them tomorrow.

All she needed was for Justin St John to give her a little leeway. Once having drawn him into her power, she was not going to let him get away from her. Not, at least, until she had given him the full treatment.

Kelly hid her nervous apprehension with bustling efficiency as she set her other patient up in the traction unit.

She hoped Justin St John was not going to be difficult. He needed physiotherapy. She wanted to give it to him. But what he wanted was another question altogether. She took several deep breaths before returning to the treatment room where she had left him.

The knots in her stomach loosened slightly when she found him stretched out on the table and stripped to his shirt and underwear. Kelly was grateful that he had kept the shirt on. It was difficult enough to view him with any kind of objectivity. She didn't need the distraction of having too much of his physique on full view. The memory of how his body had felt against hers last night was distraction enough.

She stared down at his bared legs for several moments before she plucked up the courage to touch him. 'I'm going to do extensions and rotations,' she said quickly. 'You must tell me when I hurt you. Otherwise I won't know what is causing the pain.'

She placed one hand on his hip, the other under the knee. The muscles of his stomach flinched. 'I'm sorry. I didn't mean to hurt you,' she said in alarm.

'You didn't hurt,' he grated.

Kelly closed her eyes. This was much harder to do than she had ever imagined. Yet, to Kelly, the pleasure and challenge of her profession was the diagnostic work involved.

She took Justin St John's leg through the range of movement that was allowable. In her mind's eye she imagined the muscles stretching and contracting around the joint until the pain became severe. She did not stop until she was certain she had an accurate picture of what was going on inside his body.

Because he had favoured the leg, there had been some muscle atrophy. A lot of work was needed to bring it back to what it should be. If only Justin St John would co-operate...

Kelly opened her eyes, fired with new zeal for the task of making him completely whole again. She found Justin St John's gaze fixed on her with unwavering intensity, and a self-conscious flush swept into her cheeks. She tried to think how to explain what she was doing, and gave up the attempt almost straight away.

'You haven't been looking after that leg properly, have you?' she said quietly. 'And I don't mean this last week. You've been neglecting it for years.'

His mouth twisted. He met the challenge in her eyes with a hard, mocking look. 'There are other things in life that interest me more,' he said drily.

The way he looked at her made her wonder what had been going through his mind while she was manipulating his leg with her eyes closed. If he'd been remembering...

Kelly's heart skipped a beat. She had to remember what they were here for.

'If you keep on the way you've been going,' it will only cause you more and more trouble,' she admonished him. 'Already there's some wasting in the adductor muscles. Don't you care about yourself?'

He grimaced and turned his head away before muttering a reply. 'I can put up with it.'

'Well, I won't!' Kelly protested, impatient with his attitude. 'And I'm going to fix it as best as it can be fixed. I'm going to give you back two perfect legs.'

Again he gave her that intense, inscrutable look. 'Why should you care?' he asked softly.

Kelly had the feeling that she was walking across quicksand, and any moment she was going to be sucked in. 'Because I know I can do it…and I want to,' she answered slowly, but she knew there was more to it than that. Somehow she sensed that the leg was a barrier between them, and she had a strong instinctive urge to break down that barrier. And any others he raised. She saw the flicker of dissatisfaction with her reply, felt his withdrawal. 'Perhaps it's because I can't stand to see anyone in pain,' she added more forcefully. 'Certainly not in unnecessary pain.'

His shoulders lifted and fell in a careless little shrug. 'Two years of operations and exercises left me with a distaste for spending any more time on the problem. The leg was never going to be good enough to stand up to much, anyway. So I rechannelled my career into an area where it didn't matter. The pain only flares up occasionally. After I've done something stupid,' he added self-mockingly.

Like chasing her, Kelly thought guiltily. She quickly applied the suction cups for the interferential. 'You've got too many years ahead of you to let your leg deteriorate,' she scolded. 'You're still a young man.'

He made a contemptuous sound.

Kelly felt even more impatient with him. 'I'll bet you're not even old enough to have a hip replacement,' she said scornfully. And that was information that she really did want to know. 'How old are you, anyway?' she demanded.

'Old enough to know better, Kelly Hanrahan.'

The low growl had a distinct bite to it.

Kelly took the bull by the horns. 'If you're going to keep on kissing me, I want to know how old you are.'

She heard the swift intake of his breath. His body went curiously rigid. He said nothing.

The silence seemed to go on and on.

Kelly was quite certain he was not going to answer. Apparently he had no intention of kissing her ever again. The disappointment she felt was acute enough to make her feel silly and miserable. She started to turn away.

'How old do you have to be to have a hip replacement?'

Kelly glared at him, resenting the diversionary tactic, but his eyes were hooded, revealing nothing of his thoughts or feelings. His face wore an abstracted look.

'Generally they don't like to do them until a person is forty,' she replied tartly.

The silence lasted for fifteen or twenty seconds. 'Then I've only got two more years to go,' he said at last.

Kelly's spirits instantly lifted and she sighed with satisfaction as she worked out the arithmetic. Sixteen years between them didn't form an unbridgeable gap. A man of thirty-eight was considered in his prime, and women always matured more quickly than men. By her reckoning, that just about put them on a par. There was certainly nothing wrong about her feeling attracted to him or him feeling attracted to her.

She smiled triumphantly as she switched on the machine. 'I want you to relax now and let the interferential do its work. I'm going to attend to some of my other patients. If you have any trouble, just give me a yell,' she said, and even she could hear the exultant lilt in her voice.

Justin St John was starting to bend!

CHAPTER SEVEN

ALTHOUGH Kelly was satisfied that she had won the honours in the first round with Justin St John, it was early days yet, and the end was still very much up in the air. Why had he changed his mind from yesterday, when he had categorically refused any more physiotherapy from her? Why hadn't he attacked her about stealing Rasputin? He hadn't even mentioned it. He had to have some plan up his sleeve.

Kelly conscientiously carried through the exercises necessary for her other patient, but she was extremely aware of Justin St John's presence in the next room. However, with the extra workload that his presence had thrust on her, she was kept busy for the next forty minutes.

Not that he suffered in any way from the lack of her personal attention. Leaving the machine on him for that long wouldn't do any harm, and could only do good. The high frequency waves would help relieve the pain. The low frequency waves would exercise and help correct the atrophy of the underused muscles.

After she had finished with two other patients, she could give Justin St John her undivided attention until ten-thirty. And that would be the danger period. Kelly was aware that if he was going to make some counterstroke against her it would be during this time that it came.

The minutes rolled by all too quickly.

Kelly returned to the cubicle.

For a moment she felt light-headed, much the same as she felt before the penultimate round in a Grand Prix event, when it was essential not only to do well, but to pull out something special that would place her in front of all the other competitors. She took a deep breath and pulled the curtain shut behind her.

She switched off the interferential and removed the suction cups. 'How does this feel now?'

'Better,' he grunted.

'I'll finish off with some resisted exercises and then some ultrasound.'

He complied with all her instructions without complaint. No conversation was entered into by either party as she made him move his leg against the pressure of her hand. But there was a distinct rise of tension in the room. The physical connection that the exercises demanded engendered a very personal sense of intimacy.

'That's enough for today,' Kelly finally said, her voice made husky by a tightened throat. She swallowed hard, then attempted a brisker tone. 'To do any more might stir it up. But when we can get more freedom of movement I'll start you on the weights. I want you here every day...'

'Kelly...'

He levered himself up on his elbows and it was a demand to meet his gaze. She looked up, knowing and expecting this to be the moment of reckoning. There was a sardonic twist to his mouth, and the grey eyes were hard and probing.

Kelly's chin lifted belligerently. 'If it's beneath your dignity to come here, I'll come to you.'

He shook his head. 'You can't really believe you can barter therapy for the horses...'

'I wouldn't try!' A flush of indignation highlighted her cheeks. 'And that's a very offensive comment! I've given you no reason to relate the two things in such a cynical fashion. I do care about you, whether you want me to or not. And I don't want to see you...incapacitated, when it's all so unnecessary.'

His lips curled with bitter irony. 'If I hadn't been incapacitated, you wouldn't have got away from me yesterday evening.'

Kelly took a deep breath and faced him squarely. 'If your feelings were more human, it wouldn't have been necessary for me to get away from you. You would let me ride my horses. I wouldn't have to steal them from you.' Her green eyes blazed with righteous conviction. 'You're the one who is unjust. I'm sorry about the pain you inflicted upon yourself, but it's all your own fault.'

He rose up from the table, every line of his face drawn into haughty reserve. 'If I were less of a human being, I would give you every encouragement to break your foolish neck. The thought of having to deliver such news to your grandfather is sufficient inducement by itself to make me decide that you should not ride my horses. I . . .'

'Don't bring my grandfather into this. Yesterday it was Noni. Today . . .'

'It's for your own good.'

'No, it's not. It's . . .'

'I also wish to apologise for kissing you. With our age difference, it was a totally foolish thing to do.'

'There's no need to apologise,' Kelly insisted hotly. 'As kisses go, that was an experience worth having.'

His face tightened. 'We're not getting anywhere with this.' He eased himself off the table and walked to the chair where he had hung his trousers. He kept his back turned to her as he effected a more dignified appearance.

Hating his silence, Kelly plunged on to another tack. 'I haven't thanked you for returning my car. I appreciated the consideration. In fact . . .'

'Simple expedience!' he cut in brusquely. 'It would have been more of a problem to me if you'd presented yourself at Marian Park for another session of plea-bargaining.'

He swung around, formidable in his armoured control. 'You're a very forward young woman, Kelly Hanrahan,' he stated with an emphasis that had Kelly instantly bristling. 'But I will make a bargain with you,' he added in a tone that smacked of condescension.

Her temperature soared. He'd forced all the running, not her! 'You're an impossibly arrogant man, Justin St John,' she shot back at him recklessly. 'And I'm not sure I want to make a bargain with you. If you're going to pretend nothing happened between us...'

'I'll tell you what's between us,' he whipped back bitterly. 'About fifteen years. And a matter of horses. And it wouldn't be the first time a woman used her body to get what she wants.'

That he could have interpreted her response to him in such a way shocked and angered Kelly. For several moments she was utterly speechless, colour ebbing and flowing in her cheeks. He watched her with hard, remorseless eyes as she struggled to bring herself under control.

'You can leave now, Mr St John. You have had your treatment. If you're not in a medical fund, that will be twenty dollars,' she bit out, then marched off to the desk in the waiting-room to do whatever paperwork was required to send him on his way.

She heard him follow her with his walking-stick, but scorned to look up until he reached the opposite side of her desk. Then she raised a frosty glare. 'I hope you appreciate how much better you're walking on that leg?'

'Yes,' he replied curtly, and the steely grey eyes met and returned her challenge. 'How long will it take to restore it to perfect working order?'

'I don't make God-like judgements!' she snapped, too furious to feel any triumph that he was considering her advice. 'After regular therapy for a fortnight, I might be able to give you a fairly accurate prognosis. Will nine o'clock each day suit you?'

'I'll make it suit!'

He dropped a twenty-dollar note on the desk. Kelly did not bother picking it up. She wrote out a receipt, her biro stabbing at the paper in her fierce resentment.

'I won't be here next week,' she informed him as she banged down her pen, tore the page out of the receipt-book and handed it to him with icy disdain. 'But I'll leave instructions for your treatment with my replacement.'

He ignored the receipt. 'Why won't you be here?' he demanded, his eyes boring into hers.

'Because I'll be show-jumping,' she stated defiantly.

His hand whipped out and caught her around the wrist. 'Not on that black stallion!'

Her eyes flared with immovable determination. 'No matter what you do about Rasputin, I'll still go show-jumping. I've been offered other rides, and if I have to take what I can get, I will! You can't stop me!'

His fingers tightened around her wrist. 'Bring that black rogue back, Kelly, and I'll reconsider about the other horses.'

'Rasputin is the best! I can win more surely on him than any other horse.'

'And lose more surely!' was the fierce retort. 'No one has been able to ride him.'

Kelly bared her teeth. 'I can. Now, take your hand off mine, Mr St John. I might think you're using your body to get what you want.'

Every nerve in Kelly's body jangled in alarm as the tension between them gathered explosive proportions. Then, suddenly, the dangerous glitter in his eyes faded and he broke into a self-derisive laugh.

'Touché!' He released her wrist and regarded her with grudging admiration. 'I see I cannot impose my will on yours. But whether you want to believe it or not, I do have your best interests at heart, Kelly.'

'That's very presumptuous of you, Mr St John,' she replied, disdaining his claim. 'In case it's escaped your notice, I'm old enough to make my own decisions.'

'Then make the right one. The only sensible one!' he said in exasperation.

Another patient came through the door.

'Please . . . reconsider.'

The soft appeal nearly made her change her mind. She didn't want to fight with him. She wanted to please him. If he let her ride the other three horses in exchange for Rasputin . . . but the thought of all the years of effort, Henry Lloyd's faith in her, and Noni before that...if she compromised now, it would be a betrayal in more ways than one.

Kelly couldn't do it. She lifted pained eyes, wishing he could understand. 'I'm sorry, Justin. But at present that is quite impossible.'

He looked at her steadily for a moment. Kelly could not possibly decipher what was on his mind. 'I'm sorry, too,' he said. 'I'll leave you to your patients.' He turned on his heel and walked out the door.

Kelly wondered when she would see him again—and under what circumstances. He had given her the chance to settle out of court, so to speak. Having had his offer refused, what would he do now?

Well, it was out of her control, Kelly decided. She had done the best she could by him. She could do no more.

With an air of resignation she turned to her next patient.

It was going to be a long day.

Kelly saw her last patient out of the door. Ever since Justin St John had left that morning she had been half expecting something to happen, but the rest of the day had passed without the slightest ripple out of the ordinary.

She telephoned the judge's place to check on Rasputin. Arlene Moffat assured her that he was fine; her stable-boy had set up some jumps for

Kelly, and she could come and practise any time she liked.

Kelly was tempted to drive straight out there, yet prudence dictated caution. Nothing had been resolved with Justin St John this morning, and Kelly did not think he was the type of man to tamely accept her defiance. What his next step would be, only time would tell, but Kelly did not want to risk being observed and having Rasputin taken away from her.

'I'll come out early tomorrow morning, Mrs Moffat. And many thanks to you and the judge for all you've done,' Kelly said warmly.

'Our pleasure, Kelly. And if you bring your clothes for work, you can shower and change here. That will save you some time.'

Kelly thanked her once more, and with her spirits boosted by the thought of having her favourite horse to ride again she locked up the office and went home.

Justin St John's next move stared her in the face as she drove up to the house. The palomino, the chestnut and the grey were all tethered to the fence railing.

When she could tear her eyes away from the horses, she saw her grandfather strolling down the veranda steps, wearing a huge grin on his face. Kelly's heart pounded with excitement and uncertainty as she stopped the car and leapt out.

'How did they get here, Grandpa?'

'Stable-hand brought them down about half an hour ago.'

Kelly shook her head, trying to work out the implications. 'What does it mean?' she wondered out loud, unable to believe that Justin St John had completely climbed down from his position, but wildly hoping that he had.

'It means you can ride them and jump them to your heart's content,' her grandfather rolled out with relish. 'And I've put your saddle on Rapunzel because I reckoned you'd want to take her out first.'

'But . . . surely the stable-hand said something?' Kelly cried, bursting to know the best . . . or the worst.

'No more than I've told you.'

'Nothing about Rasputin?'

'Not a word!' Her grandfather grinned again. 'Reckon he's capitulated, Kelly.'

The Justin St Johns of the world did not capitulate, she thought grimly. Yet he seemed to have accepted her advice about the physiotherapy he needed. Completely perplexed by the man, Kelly looked at her grandfather for his advice.

'Don't look three gift horses in the mouth, Kelly,' he said with an encouraging chuckle. 'Go to it, girl. Who knows what might happen next?'

'That's true enough!' Kelly said with feeling. 'I'll go and get changed.'

'Just like old times,' her grandfather said with happy satisfaction.

But it couldn't be quite the same without Rasputin. And Kelly wasn't at all sure what game Justin St John was playing with this open-handed gesture. Or was it a trick? she wondered as she stripped off her work clothes and pulled on her riding gear.

Perhaps it was his way of pressuring her to accept the bargain he had offered this morning. Showing her his good faith, and expecting her to respond with the return of Rasputin. If so, he could think again, Kelly determined stubbornly. As far as she was concerned, there were no strings attached. And she would play it that way until otherwise informed.

She took all three horses down to the practice field. She set the grey and the chestnut free to graze while she gave the palomino a work-out over the jumps. Rapunzel was willing enough, and game, but she didn't have the black stallion's ability in jumping. Nevertheless, Kelly enjoyed encouraging the good-natured mare. When she managed all the jumps without knocking a rail, Kelly laughed from sheer elation.

It was then that she saw the man watching her from the fence which edged the pine forest. Although he was too far away for Kelly to discern his features, she knew instinctively that it was Justin St John. Still exuberant over her success with Rapunzel, Kelly waved to him.

He did not wave back.

Kelly was tempted to ride up to him, but even from this distance there was a forbidding look about him which suggested she wouldn't be welcomed. He was probably watching to see if she broke her foolish neck, Kelly decided. It would support her cause more if she kept on riding and showed him how wrong he was.

He watched her until she had taken all three horses through their paces. When she started to lead them up towards the stables, he moved away from the fence and disappeared into the pine forest, making it very clear that he had nothing more to say to her at this time.

Kelly smothered her disappointment with the hope that he would keep his nine o'clock appointment in her office tomorrow. Having seen how capable a horse-woman she was, perhaps he would be more reasonable about Rasputin.

Arlene Moffat echoed the same opinion when Kelly related the latest developments over the Moffats' breakfast-table the next morning. The black stallion had performed like a dream for her, and Kelly's resolve not to part with him had been immeasurably hardened by the morning's ride.

However, when Justin St John entered her office at five minutes to nine, he carried a distinctly unapproachable air with him.

'Good morning,' he said, coolly polite. 'Same room?'

'Yes,' said Kelly, choking up from his hard unrelenting manner. Why couldn't he smile at her?

It wasn't until he was on the table, ready for more treatment, that she screwed up the courage to speak again. 'Thank you for letting me have the horses back,' she rushed out.

The grey eyes stabbed at her. 'I don't want your thanks. You know my feelings on the matter. It was simply the lesser of two evils,' he stated curtly.

He didn't mention Rasputin.

Kelly didn't either, deciding that discretion was the better part of valour on that sore point.

He watched her ride again that afternoon... a dark, brooding figure leaning on the fence, waiting for her to have an accident. Kelly rode particularly well, controlling every move of her mount with exhilarating ease. She liked Justin St John watching her. It lent a marvellous sharpness to every moment.

Eventually he would bend, she kept telling herself. He cared about her, just as she cared about him. She was certain of it.

Judge Moffat's car was parked outside the house when she got home. It was chess night again. Kelly heard her grandfather's voice raised in umbrage as she crossed the veranda, and wondered what had upset him. She hurried into the kitchen where the two men were sitting over their supper.

'What are you on about, Grandpa?' she asked. He had obviously worked himself up about something.

'Kelly, I took the lambs up to Mrs Ryan this afternoon, just like I always do. She said Justin St John didn't want more than four each week any more. That he wanted some beef for a change.' His eyes almost smoked with outrage. 'I'm going to have to run beef-cattle with the sheep!'

Kelly frowned. 'Maybe he doesn't understand the agreement, Grandpa,' she suggested in soft appeasement.

'Herefords or Charalais or Santa Gertrudis...'

'What if he develops a taste for chicken?' the judge put in with sympathetic concern. 'What are you going to do then?'

'Chicken?' her grandfather squawked.

'Or fish?' the judge added.

It was the final straw! 'Henry Lloyd ate lamb for seventy-five years,' Michael O'Reilly thundered. 'If it was good enough for Henry Lloyd, it's good enough for Justin St John!'

'Quite right,' the judge agreed. 'He's got to be taught to fit in. This is sheep country. Always has been. Always will be. He can't come in here changing things. We've got to stand up to him. Show him he's wrong!'

'I'll have a word with him when he comes for his physiotherapy tomorrow, Grandpa,' Kelly offered. 'I'm sure he doesn't understand.'

'You haven't got him to understand about Rasputin, Kelly,' the judge warned pessimistically, then switched his attention back to her grandfather. 'And talking about sheep, Michael, I've had a thought about Octavian Augustus the Fourth...'

'It's clear that Justin St John doesn't really appreciate sheep,' Michael grumbled. 'Let's go into the living-room and set up the chess-board, Judge. I'm in a fighting mood tonight.'

Kelly wondered if her grandfather remembered his intention to let the judge win this time, but she didn't get a chance to remind him. In fact, she was so tired after her long day that she went to bed before the chess match was over and didn't hear the final outcome that evening.

However, when she had finished with Rasputin the next morning, Judge Moffat took great pride in telling her that he had swept her grandfather off the chess-board.

Kelly wished it could be as easy to checkmate Justin St John.

He arrived for his physiotherapy with the same stiff-necked reserve he had worn the previous day. Kelly decided she would not be put off or put down or put out again, no matter how he acted or what he said or how he made her feel. Nevertheless, she worked on her composure while he was on the interferential, and waited until she had started the resisted exercises before opening her account.

'You've got my grandfather upset again, Justin. You're not keeping to the agreement.'

He groaned.

'Did I hurt you?' Kelly asked anxiously.

'No. And I don't recall giving you permission to call me Justin,' he said peevishly.

'You call me Kelly,' she argued. 'Why shouldn't I call you Justin?'

He sighed. 'How have I upset your grandfather?'

'You didn't take all the lambs you're supposed to,' she explained. 'Under the agreement...'

'I'm sick to death of eating lamb!'

'You don't have to eat it yourself. You could give it away. Or sell it to the butcher,' Kelly suggested brightly. 'But you've got to take them. Henry Lloyd used to...'

'I am not Henry Lloyd!' He glared at her. 'And I'm sick to death of being told what Henry Lloyd used to do.'

Kelly closed her mouth in thin-lipped disapproval. She glared back at Justin St John. The tension in the room thickened. He bent first.

'All right! Tell me what Henry Lloyd used to do,' he said in weary disgust.

'He used to pass the lamb on to his staff when he didn't need it for himself. The gardeners and...'

'Fine! I'll pass it on.'

Kelly heaved a sigh of satisfaction. 'I told Grandpa you'd understand. He was having visions of having to run cattle to cater for your taste. Herefords and...'

'You can't mean it?' Justin levered himself up on his elbows with a look of sheer incredulity.

'Well, what else could he do? If you wouldn't take the full complement of lambs according to the agreement...'

'Never mind!' He shook his head and dropped down on to the table again. He breathed deeply for several seconds. 'Assure your grandfather that any agreement will be kept to the letter from now on.'

'Thank you,' she said, even though he didn't like to be thanked. He should be more gracious about that, Kelly thought to herself. But she didn't want to criticise him too severely, because she had another favour to ask him.

She waited until the exercises were completed and was spreading oil over his hip-joint in preparation for the ultrasound.

'Is it all right if I take the horse-truck?' she asked, her eyes pleading her need. 'I can't transport the horses without it.'

He closed his eyes against her and his jaw tightened as if he was clenching his teeth. 'You haven't brought back that damned stallion yet,' he bit out.

Kelly took a deep breath. 'Would you let me ride him if I did?'

'No!' It was a hard, explosive negative, leaving her no room to manoeuvre.

'Well, that settles that,' she reasoned quietly. 'But if I'm to compete with the other horses, I can't get them to Dapto without the horse-truck.'

'Kelly...' His voice sounded very strained. She felt his flesh quiver under her hand. 'Will you stop spreading that oil and get on with it?'

'Oh!' Flustered by her hand's dalliance, Kelly snatched it away and grabbed for the ultrasound. She played the small machine over his muscles as she struggled to regain her composure.

It wasn't easy. She was more aware of him than ever. It was even worse when she had to switch the ultrasound off and wipe the oil from his skin with the tissues. She felt quite sure he didn't want her to touch him.

'You can get up now,' she choked out, and quickly turned away to dispose of the used tissues.

Every pore in her body was listening for him to get off the table and walk to the chair where he had hung his trousers. Every nerve was stretched tight, waiting for a less discomfiting distance between them.

His feet thudded softly on to the floor. The short ensuing silence pulsed with a tension that was not wholly hers. The urge to turn around and see what he was feeling was terribly strong. But he had called her a forward young woman, and even suggested she could be using her body to get what she wanted. If he thought she had been caressing him knowingly...

There was a whispering sigh, and at last footsteps moving away. Kelly's chest hurt from holding her breath. She let it out slowly, desperately trying to regain some control of the situation.

'You can take the truck. As long as you don't take Rasputin.'

The flat words slapped Kelly's mind into refocusing on the problem of her favourite horse. She couldn't go without him. He was her best chance of winning the main event.

Justin St John finished dressing and swung around, his eyes stabbing right into her heart and soul as he spoke with relentless decision. 'Promise me you won't slip him in along the way. Promise me that now, Kelly.'

Slowly she shook her head. 'No! You're wrong about this. Terribly wrong. As you've been about so many other things.'

His face contorted with angry frustration. 'Why do you have to be so stubborn? You're a beautiful young woman. With your whole life ahead of you. Why put it at risk?'

'All life is a risk!' she retorted. 'And show-jumping is no more dangerous than playing polo. You did that, didn't you? And I bet if you could have gone on playing it after your accident, you would have done that too.'

'But I couldn't. And I didn't.' His eyes glittered over her with intense bitterness. 'And I don't want to see the same thing happen to you.'

Kelly flushed at the unwitting cruelty of her words. 'I'm sorry. It's just that . . .'

'You think I'm unreasonable,' he mocked savagely. 'Well, let me tell you, Kelly Hanrahan, I was riding horses before you were born. And my sister was in show-jumping. I'm very familiar with all types of horses, and I've seen Rasputin's kind before.' His mouth twisted. 'Noni Lloyd had one just like him. A Hanoverian stallion. Bred for jumping. He'd rather crash into a fence than balk. One mistake from you, Kelly—cutting him too short to gain time, not getting him set into the right stride for a triple or a combination—and he'll go for it anyway. And he'll take you with him.'

'You don't know Rasputin,' Kelly defended. 'He can adjust. Improvise. He's a natural. There's no other horse like him.'

A bleak weariness settled in the grey eyes. 'Kelly, I can't stop you from show-jumping other owners' horses, but I can stop you from competing with mine. I don't want it to come to that. Please...reconsider. You can ride the other three if you must. But not Rasputin.'

'You don't understand,' Kelly pleaded. 'I'll never find another like him. To ride Rasputin...it's like magic...'

'Black magic!' he snapped impatiently. 'You're tempting the gods every time you mount that devil. Put an end to it before he puts an end to you. Make your mind up to that, Kelly. For your own sake!'

There was no talking to him. She could see that. And he wouldn't even give her the chance to prove him wrong. While she was still floundering for a way to reach out to him, he pulled out his wallet, extracted a twenty-dollar note, and dropped it on the table.

'Think about it!' he said harshly, and walked out.

CHAPTER EIGHT

KELLY did think about what Justin St John had said.

But he was wrong!

She kept on riding the three horses each afternoon. He never missed watching her. It saddened Kelly that there was more than a fence dividing them. She wished that he could watch her with pleasure, that he could share the joy of it with her. But whatever compulsion drove him to watch through the whole practice session Kelly knew intuitively that it had more to do with his obsession about her safety than anything else.

And every morning she wished he could see her on Rasputin as they soared over the jumps at the judge's place. She and Rasputin understood each other. The big stallion knew what he could do and so did she. What Justin St John was trying to force upon her was totally unfair.

After much agonising over his ultimatum, Kelly came to the only decision that seemed right to her.

'I thought you said you'd be away this week,' Justin remarked one morning as he was paying for his physiotherapy treatment. For the first time Kelly saw a hint of uncertainty in the probing grey eyes.

'I have no way of taking all the horses, so I've had to cancel my entries to the minor events,' she said flatly.

'Kelly...' He heaved a sigh of exasperation.

She took a deep breath and looked him straight in the eye. 'I won't lie to you, or go behind your back, Justin. The Dapto Grand Prix is scheduled for Saturday afternoon. It's a qualifying round of the Swan Premium Pacific League of the World Cup. Rasputin is entered and I'm taking him.'

His face went grim.

Kelly's heart sank to a new low. She tried to deliver her challenge with undaunted spirit, but tears wobbled in her eyes as she spoke the fateful words. 'I know you have the power to stop us from competing. But you could at least watch Rasputin in action first, before you take him away from me.'

He shook his head, stared at her with pained eyes, then walked out, leaving her with no answer either way. Kelly didn't know what he would do. Perhaps he didn't know himself.

She did not have the heart to ride that afternoon. Or the next. The contest of wills with Justin St John had drained her natural energy and, having limited herself to Rasputin for the Dapto Show, she concentrated solely on him.

Justin St John made no comment on her decision, nor on her failure to exercise the other horses. She did not even see him on Friday. Roy Farley telephoned to cancel the appointment. No excuse was offered.

She rose early on Saturday morning, not having slept well at all. Her grandfather insisted she eat a good breakfast, then waved her off with the admonishment, 'You can show him, Kelly!'

'If he gives me the chance,' she replied with an unhappy grimace.

'He would have told you by now if he was going to stop you,' her grandfather reasoned.

Kelly tried to be optimistic as she drove to the judge's place. When she arrived there she was greeted by more good wishes and encouragement. Judge Moffat helped her load Rasputin into his horse-float, and Arlene insisted on giving her a picnic basket for lunch.

The trip to Dapto passed without incident. The showground area set aside for the equestrians' use was heavily populated with horse-trucks and caravans. Being a latecomer, Kelly had to park where she could, which was a fair distance from the arena. Not that it mattered. She didn't really feel like being in the thick of things.

Kelly spent what was left of the morning grooming Rasputin, plaiting his mane and using a comb and plastic template to pattern the glossy coat of his rump. She was not left alone for long. Other riders on the show-jumping circuit spotted her and came over to chat. She deflected any questions about her present situation and steered the conversations towards what had happened in the events she had missed.

She did not see Justin St John.

Two hours prior to the Grand Prix, she checked at the post entry office to make sure her entry was still valid. It was. She did a nervous scan of the stands, hoping, fearing, to see Justin seated somewhere among the spectators, but there was no one who looked anything like him.

The ballot was drawn for the first-round Order of Go. Kelly and Rasputin were placed third to last to take the field. Kelly was quite pleased to be placed well down in the order. It gave her the opportunity to see how tough her competition would be on the day.

She took Rasputin off for a ride around the grounds to settle him down. The excitement of having all the other horses around always made him jumpy. He seemed to sense a big event, and wanted to show off his supremacy.

Kelly did her best to quell her own nerves too, but she could not help thinking this might be the last time she ever rode the great stallion. And, if it was to be a worthy swan-song, they had to win.

She heard the announcement of the event over the loudspeakers and returned to a vantage point from where she could watch the other riders in action. Her gaze flicked once more over the spectators in the stands, and her heart leapt into her mouth when she saw him climbing the steps to the main grandstand.

He had come! He was going to watch!

Kelly was barely conscious of what was happening in the arena. Horse followed horse. She had no idea who was doing well or how many had gone clear rounds. Her turn came.

'Rasputin...ridden by Kelly Hanrahan,' boomed over the loudspeaker.

She rode the black stallion to the starting position, her heart hammering with the need to show Justin how good Rasputin was, how good she was, how good they were together.

And up in the grandstand, Justin St John shifted forward on the wooden bench seat, too tense to remain still. He felt sick to his stomach. He kept telling himself that Kelly was as fine a rider as he had ever seen, that it couldn't happen again ... that she had the right to live her life how she wanted. But she looked so small on that great black horse, small and fragile, her body all too easily smashed.

The announcer was reeling out Rasputin's recent achievements, sparking interest: 'An exciting horse...a great crowd-pleaser...very strong competitor...'

Justin's hands clenched as Kelly was given the starting signal. He could hardly bear to watch as she urged the black stallion towards the first hurdle, yet he couldn't bear not to watch. His body half lifted with them, and he only breathed again when they took the jump cleanly.

They flew over each set of rails, and took the spread fence in their stride. Rasputin pranced impatiently as Kelly set him for the combination, then soared over the double with consummate ease. He disposed of the next three fences with seemingly contemptuous arrogance, but Justin tensed again as they turned for the 'Liverpool Ditch'.

Several horses and riders had come to grief at the Liverpool—a short white picket fence preceding the water and the fence behind it. There had been two quite nasty falls when horses had balked at the obstacle. If Rasputin acknowledged an obstacle at all, it was not discernible. He sailed over without the slightest hint of a falter.

Only the single rail to go before the triple which had brought half the field down—two sets of rails and the brick wall, each jump escalating in height and no room for mistakes. Justin could feel his heart thundering as they leapt the single rail and lined up for the triple. Kelly held Rasputin back for a moment, harnessing the surge of power in the huge stallion before letting him go. He fired, taking all three jumps with such graceful brilliance that it brought a spontaneous burst of applause from the crowd.

A clear round.

Justin sagged in relief. When he had time to recollect himself, he wiped the perspiration from his brow and tried to review the performance he had just seen without any emotional prejudice.

The timing on each jump had been perfect. There was no doubting Rasputin's ability, nor the understanding between horse and rider. Certainly Kelly appeared to be in control of her mount. But Justin could not rid himself of the fear that the black stallion's temperament might overpower her at a critical moment.

The second round began.

By the time it came to Kelly's turn, four other riders had completed two clear rounds, so she knew there would be a jump-off to decide the place-getters. And she knew she needed a clear round to be in it. But she wasn't nervous any more. She had shown Justin. Nothing could have been more perfect than Rasputin's first round, and he was rearing to go again.

Their second round was equally faultless.

The course was changed for the jump-off. Several fences were eliminated, and the triple reduced to one set of rails and the brick wall. It wasn't simply a matter of going clear now, it was a race against the clock as well. Kelly had an advantage in being the last competitor. She would know what time she had to beat in order to win.

The first horse knocked the single rail down.

The second horse dragged the top bricks off the wall.

The third blundered on the first hurdle, too anxious to get off to a flying start.

While he wished no harm to any horse or rider, Justin prayed that the next competitor would collect jumping faults also. Then Kelly would only need a clear round on Rasputin, with no necessity to race the clock.

The fourth rider was on a magnificent grey Andalusian horse, and from the start he attacked the course with speed and purposeful control. The horse rattled a rail of the spread fence. Justin held his breath, willing it to fall, but it stayed up. A hoof rapped the top of the wall, but not a brick fell. The time was formidable. Thirty-six point nine seconds!

Justin buried his face in his hands.

He knew Kelly would go for it. He knew that damned black stallion would go for it. And he couldn't watch.

He couldn't. Yet he had to!

Kelly instantly replotted her course, minimising the distance between jumps. Distance was time! She needed controlled pacing more than speed. It was risky, but if she was to win... and Rasputin had the ability to do it.

She stroked his neck. His ears pricked back. 'This is the test, my beauty,' she crooned softly. 'Let's show him we're the best!'

Rasputin snorted.

They were given the starting signal. Kelly dug her heels in and Rasputin surged into his long, powerful stride. The first two fences blurred by. She wheeled the big stallion quickly and drove him over the spread, turned sharply, then took the single rail at an angle so she could cut across to the 'Liverpool Ditch'. It was a daring move, but Rasputin responded without turning a hair. He motored through the combination and charged down to round the corner for the last set of rails and the wall.

Conscious of the seconds ticking away, Kelly urged him on to the rails too fast. She knew it— could feel him overstretching. The wall was going to be too close for his normal stride. As he landed, she gave a sharp tug on the reins. He couldn't instantly check his momentum, but he knew what she wanted . . . saw what had to be done. He managed a shorter stride and climbed, surging off his back legs, lifting in a great, hooping leap that carried them both up and over the wall.

A thrill of sheer exultation rippled through Kelly's body. They had done it. She waited for the official time, but she knew they had done it even before the announcement came—thirty-three point two seconds!

She jumped off and hugged Rasputin. He was a true champion. Justin had to recognise it now. Only a champion could have taken the wall as Rasputin had. Justin would have to admit it. And everything would be all right between them.

She looked up to where he had been sitting in the grandstand, but people were moving around and she couldn't see him. Maybe he was making his way down to her, she thought happily. He surely wouldn't leave without saying something to her.

The other riders congratulated her and complimented her on a great ride. The officials called the place-getters into the ring to present the ribbons. Kelly proudly mounted Rasputin again and led the other horses in. The blue ribbon was hung around his neck and Kelly received the winner's cheque.

But, as marvellous as winning was, she was filled with impatience for the ceremony to be over so that she could meet up with Justin.

At last they were allowed to move out. Kelly's head swivelled around in search of the man she wanted to see, but he was nowhere in sight.

She wanted to share her triumph with him. She was sure that, given the chance, there were a lot of things they could share if Justin St John could only learn to be more reasonable.

Furthermore, it justified her actions.

And, since he didn't seem to be coming to her, Kelly decided she had to find him, find out what was really on his mind, get the situation between them resolved once and for all.

CHAPTER NINE

As URGENT as she felt about looking for Justin St John, Kelly couldn't push through the milling crowd on Rasputin. Nor could she simply dismount and leave the big stallion uncared for, particularly when he had risen to the occasion with such great heart and skill. She rode him back to the float, tethered him on a long lead and gave him a bale of hay to nibble as a reward.

She took off her riding helmet and tossed it into the car, then ran her fingers through her hair, wishing she had time to brush it, but too anxious to delay any longer. She wanted to find Justin before he left. Hoping she was not already too late, she set off towards the exit gate.

'Kelly...'

The timbre of the voice was harsh and strained, but unmistakably Justin St John's. Kelly swung around and saw him striding between two caravans, moving purposefully towards her. Her face lit with pleasure. He had not deserted her. He had come after her.

She laughed and ran to him, flinging her arms around his neck in happiness and relief. 'I thought you'd gone,' she said breathlessly, her eyes shining up at him. 'But you saw him, didn't you? You saw how good he was, and...'

Justin St John didn't hear a word of what Kelly was saying. Her lovely face was vividly alive. Her body was warm and vibrant against his. His hands moved automatically to press her closer to him, to run over the sweet curves of her body, to savour the touch of flesh and bone that were still wonderfully intact.

Kelly's excited rush of words dried up when she saw he wasn't listening to her. The grey eyes seemed dazed. And she was suddenly very conscious of the way he was moulding her body to his, slowly gathering her closer and closer, his hands roving over her with a sensuous deliberation that set her pulse skittering.

The stretch material of her riding-pants was like a second skin, and Kelly felt that what he was doing was terribly intimate. She shouldn't really allow it, not in public view, although a quick glance assured her that no one around her was interested. And, while it might not be very sensible, she did not want to pull away from him. Nevertheless, her heart started a wild hammering as his hold on her tightened.

'Justin...' she protested weakly.

His eyes sharpened on hers, and her breath caught in her throat as she watched the intense glitter of want and need forge into a ruthless determination that swept aside everything else. His mouth took hers with a voracious passion that allowed for no questioning on her part. He swept her into a maelstrom of sensation, evoking a wild, mindless response from her, a joyous, greedy release from the tension that had blighted their relationship for so many long hours...days...weeks.

He covered her face with kisses and took her lips again and again, as if he needed to feed on the reality of her, the very breath of her life, the essence of all that she was; and the more he took the more he wanted.

Kelly was totally swamped: her body pulsing to the urgent beat of his need, exulting in it, mindlessly abandoning herself to it, her whole being caught up in the wonder of what was happening.

'I want you,' he breathed when at last he lifted his face away from hers.

Kelly opened her eyes, still dazed but intuitively grasping that Justin was saying something important, something that would change all that had previously happened between them.

His eyes burned with resolution, and when he spoke his voice throbbed with need and purpose. 'I want you to marry me.'

Kelly was so stunned, she could barely believe she had heard him correctly. 'Marry you?'

His mouth curled into a sardonic smile. 'Yes. Marry me. Be my wife. Give me a child. At least then I'll have something to balance the rest.'

'Justin...' Kelly shook her head, still finding his proposal too startling to accept. 'We haven't known each other very long. And most of the time we've been fighting...'

His eyes mocked her. 'Do you want to pretend that there's nothing between us?' The pointed reminder of her accusation against him hit home, and to drive it even further home he softly added, 'Something special! If I were making love to you right now, Kelly, I doubt very much that you'd be telling me to stop.'

She flushed. 'That's a dreadful assumption,' she murmured, feeling too uncomfortable about his supposition to admit he was right. After all, she was not in the habit of taking lovers.

His smile was all irony.

Her hands fluttered up in a gesture of helplessness. 'I can't deny I'm very attracted to you. And there has been something...even that first day when...when you touched my cheek as if...' She searched for words to express how he had affected her. 'I had the feeling...that you weren't a stranger. That...'

Her eyes lifted to question his, and it disturbed her to see a shadow of reserve slide over his face, as if he had something to hide from her. Or was she expressing something he didn't feel at all? He said he wanted her. Maybe it was only a physical thing for him.

She shook her head. 'I simply don't know you well enough to say that I love you, Justin. And marriage without love...'

His face hardened. 'All life is a risk! You said that yourself, Kelly. And you're prepared to risk your life on that black stallion. What's so different about risking your life with me?'

'I'm not risking my life on Rasputin,' she protested. 'You saw...'

'I saw that but for the grace of God you would have crashed into the wall,' he cut in fiercely.

'That's not true!'

'Kelly, I'm not interested in arguing. I've made my position clear. Marry me. That's what I want. I believe that's what you want too.' His eyes bored into hers with intense urgency, as if he was willing her to agree with him.

But it was all too sudden for Kelly. A lifelong commitment needed thinking about. 'Does that mean you've changed your mind about me show-jumping?' she asked, wanting so much more than he was offering.

'No.' The negative was sharp. For a moment the grey eyes were washed with the weary bleakness she had seen in them before. He sighed, and his voice softened. 'But I won't try to stop you again.'

A dismal void opened up in her heart. 'We wouldn't share,' she said sadly.

'There are other things to share, Kelly.'

The other things shimmered between them: the physical intimacy of being husband and wife, children, Marian Park with all its gracious living...so much that could be good.

And yet Kelly sensed they would never be truly together. There was a part of Justin he would always hold back. Maybe it was the years between them...too many experiences she didn't know or would never understand because she hadn't lived those years with him. Maybe there was a woman somewhere in his past who would always be dearer to him than she could ever be. There was something...something in the shadows of his eyes that set her away from him, even as he proposed the most serious bond of all.

Did he really want this? Or was it a new ploy to get her to give up show-jumping? But why would he go so far? Kelly shook her head in bewilderment. 'I don't know. It doesn't seem right,' she replied, but without any conviction. She suddenly felt very tired. Drained.

A hard, cynical mask dropped over his face. 'There's no fool like an old fool. At my age, I should have known better.'

He released her so abruptly that Kelly almost fell. He grasped her arm, steadying her until she regained her balance, then let go again.

She looked up into savagely mocking eyes and he spoke with a cold whip-sting of pride. 'I'll give you what you want, anyway. You don't have to marry me for it.' He nodded towards Rasputin. 'Bring him home. I won't fight you any more. You can continue on precisely as you did...' his mouth curled in bitter irony '...in Henry Lloyd's time.'

Then he spun on his heel and stalked away.

Kelly desperately wanted to call him back. She bit her lips to deny the temptation as she watched him go. There was more to love than wanting. More to marriage than wanting.

She felt no triumph that he had given in to her over Rasputin. Not even satisfaction. Her heart ached with a mass of tearing uncertainties.

She wasn't sure if she hadn't hurt him badly—much more than just male pride—in not accepting his proposal. On the other hand, perhaps he had simply decided he wanted a wife. The years were passing . . . he wasn't getting any younger, and if he wanted children . . . But there had been an intensity in his manner that suggested his feelings ran more deeply than that.

Certainly he found her desirable, but as for the rest . . . Kelly wasn't sure how much he cared about her feelings. Of course, he would be well aware of the advantages he could offer any woman who married him. Maybe he thought wealth and position were inducements enough. But that didn't even begin to touch on the love Kelly had always envisaged for herself.

And yet, there was something about Justin St John that was very special. She hoped she hadn't hurt him. Kelly had the awful feeling that she might never meet anyone else who had such a powerful attraction for her. And to whom she had such a powerful attraction in return.

But marriage was such a serious step. She couldn't enter into it lightly. She felt there should have been much more in preliminary interaction between herself and Justin St John before he proposed marriage.

She walked despondently back to Rasputin and began unplaiting his mane. 'I wish I understood him as well as I understand you,' she told the black stallion.

The horse nodded sympathetically.

'At least you and I can stay together,' she said, but somehow it was hollow consolation. In an effort to regain some positive thinking, she added, 'Grandpa will be pleased. We've won everything back the way it was in Henry Lloyd's time.'

Except that wasn't completely true, and never could be true again. Henry Lloyd was dead. And she hadn't met Justin St John in Henry Lloyd's time.

CHAPTER TEN

DESPITE the afternoon's victory, Kelly's trip home was no more light-hearted than the morning's drive to Dapto.

Normally she would have been out of her mind with delight at having won a Grand Prix event, but somehow it didn't seem important any more. Although of course she was happy that there would be no more problem with Rasputin.

She stopped by the judge's place to deliver the good news. Only Arlene was at home, and Kelly found it difficult to respond to the kindly woman's avid questioning, particularly when she had to explain that Justin St John no longer objected to her riding Rasputin.

'So I'll take him home to Marian Park now, and return the judge's horse-float in the morning, if that's all right,' Kelly said. She hoped that her impatience to get on her way didn't show.

'No need for you to return it, Kelly. Ezra wants you to take the float to your grandfather's place. He told me to tell you he wanted it there tonight. He said you weren't to go home without it. So that'll work out fine. He'll bring it back.'

Kelly wondered what the judge was doing with her grandfather. It wasn't chess night. But, rather than prolong the conversation, she shrugged the question aside and took her leave.

Even before she reached Marian Park, Kelly could not help but notice that very unusual activity was going on.

A helicopter was flying over the pastures with a strong searchlight beaming over the ground it covered. She wondered if someone was lost. It seemed highly unlikely, yet two police cars passed her and Kelly found that occurrence even more mystifying.

She was stopped at the entrance to the pine forest by a man who flashed a federal badge. 'Your business here, ma'am?'

'I'm returning a horse to the stables,' Kelly replied, then quickly asked, 'What's going on?'

'Were you here earlier this afternoon?'

'No, I've been at Dapto all day. Show-jumping. What's wrong?'

'Not to worry, ma'am. Nothing to do with you. Go ahead.'

The whole place was swarming with people. Even camouflaged SAS men with sub-machine guns! Kelly was left in no doubt that a search was going on. But for whom? Or what? Even when her presence was questioned again at the stables, no one would satisfy her curiosity. They actually checked her identity by walkie-talkie with someone at the house. And she noticed several army vehicles, as well as cars which were marked 'Federal Police'.

Whatever was happening was certainly out of the local league. But to be of national concern? Kelly's imagination boggled at the thought of spies or drugs or terrorists. Not at Marian Park! The mere idea was absurd. It could not be.

With Rasputin safely put away in his old stall for the night, Kelly hurried home, hoping that her grandfather could tell her something. Or Judge Moffat. His vehicle was parked near the veranda steps, and Kelly positioned her car so that the horse-float could be easily transferred to his.

Having achieved this awkward task, she raced into the house, eager to hear some answers from her grandfather. She headed straight for the kitchen where he and Judge Moffat invariably sat over the table when they weren't playing chess.

It was a huge country kitchen, but not so countrified that it was used to house animals. Kelly came to a dead halt when she saw who was occupying the floor space between the stove and the table.

There was no mistaking his identity. He stood there with the imperious air of an emperor of his breed, clothed in the finest fleece of the whole world, the distinctive curled horns adding their unique flair to the narrow, aristocratic face; the supreme sire—Octavian Augustus the Fourth!

Kelly no longer had to be told the reason for the furore up at Marian Park. Nor for whom the search was being made. Nor why it was in the national interest that Octavian Augustus the Fourth be found without there being the slightest whisper of publicity.

He was the greatest sheep sire in the world!

But what the prize ram was doing in her kitchen was a question that sent chills down Kelly's spine. She felt a rising surge of hysteria which had to be ruthlessly suppressed.

It took a concentrated effort to tear her eyes off the ram and look at her grandfather.

His expression was decidedly shifty.

She turned her gaze on Judge Moffat. His large, florid face was not as highly coloured as usual.

'Judge,' she whispered, 'you didn't do it.'

An air of guilt hung heavily over both men.

She dragged in a deep breath.

'Kelly...' her grandfather began softly. 'Things haven't worked out quite as we expected. We were only being patriotic! That's exactly how it was. Isn't it, Judge?'

'Exactly!' the judge said decisively. 'Honour and country. They come first. We didn't think...'

'We thought if we took Octavian Augustus the Fourth...'

'Grandpa, the whole place is crawling with federal police and army helicopters!' Kelly cried, appalled that they could be so foolish as to think there wouldn't be dire consequences.

Her grandfather tried to defend himself. 'You took Rasputin...'

A horse that virtually belonged to her was one thing; a ram that was coveted by all the sheep-raising nations of the world was entirely something else! Kelly shook her head in despair. 'You men have no sense of proportion at all.'

Her grandfather still argued. 'We thought we had it planned right. The judge was going to take him home in the horse-float . . .'

'They'll check!' Kelly shrilled at him. 'They'll check everything. They even checked me coming in!'

The judge sighed. 'We suspected that. We'll have to think of something else, Michael. Having started this, we're not going to lose now.'

'We have to keep him a couple of weeks, Kelly,' her grandfather said with blustering conviction. 'Until Justin St John capitulates. We never thought there would be this amount of trouble. But you must see we've got to win now.' His eyes brightened in challenge. 'There's been more excitement around here than I've seen in a long time.'

'Never had this kind of fun when I was sitting on the bench,' the judge said in support.

Despite their bravado, Kelly sensed the underlying unease, the fear of having stepped out of their depth and pulled down forces that could very well wreak vengeance on them before the night was out.

'It wasn't Justin St John who called in the army and the SAS. He was down at Dapto with me,' she said in instinctive defence of the man who had conceded so much to her.

Her grandfather looked confused for a moment, then asked, 'He was there? Did you win?'

'Yes. And yes. Not that it matters now,' Kelly said impatiently. 'What we've got to do is figure out what's to be done about Octavian Augustus the Fourth. The longer we leave it, Grandpa, the worse it'll get. It must be costing a fortune to have all those men out there searching for what we've got right here.'

'If the worst comes to the worst, we can keep him here for a couple of weeks. They'll never think of looking in this kitchen for him,' the judge said hopefully.

'We've got to beat him, Kelly,' her grandfather pleaded.

'We've got to win,' the judge said with a hint of desperation.

A heavy silence descended on the group.

Kelly understood all too well what her grandfather and Judge Moffat were feeling. It was a matter of pride and principle not to give up, yet their goal was now clearly impossible. It was no longer a simple matter between them and Justin St John. The whole thing had escalated far beyond that.

And what was Justin feeling? She had rejected him, hurt him, and he had come home to find the king-pin of his sheep-stud missing. Injury on top of injury. Inflicted by both herself and her grandfather... after all he had done for them! It wasn't fair!

'I'll have to go to him,' she said with urgent intensity. 'Even if he doesn't understand, I've got to go to him.'

The two old men stared up at her in bewilderment.

'Go to whom?' her grandfather asked.

'Justin St John, of course,' Kelly answered tersely.

'Why should you do that?' the judge asked. 'We'll beat him. However we do it,' he insisted stubbornly.

'All we've got to do is stick together,' her grandfather staunchly declared.

Kelly supposed it was remotely possible. The Crooked Creek community was close-knit, loyal to each other, ready to stand up for their own through thick and thin. But if they managed to secrete Octavian Augustus the Fourth away, they would never be able to give him back. Not openly. And not for any bargaining, either. And that wasn't fair.

For the first time in her life, Kelly felt at cross purposes with the spirit of Crooked Creek. She didn't want Grandpa and the judge to win. The change that was taking place inside her was too profound to comprehend very easily, but she knew Justin St John was responsible for it. She hadn't meant to hurt him this afternoon, and she couldn't bear for him to be hurt any more.

On the other hand, something had to be done about Grandpa and Judge Moffat, too. Somehow she had to safeguard them from any punishment for their folly. They hadn't really meant any harm.

If Justin still wanted her, she did have something to offer...something to bargain with. Would he still want to marry her?

Kelly drew in a deep breath to counteract the quantum leap of inner agitation and spoke as persuasively as she could. 'Mr St John was very generous to me this afternoon.' She flushed at the evasion of the full truth. 'He listened to me about the lambs, Grandpa. If I can get him to listen to me again...' She sighed at the enormity of that task alone. 'What else can be done?'

The two men shook their heads. They were not impressed by the idea of her interceding for them. But they were unable to come up with any alternative suggestions that might get them out of trouble. They stared down at Octavian Augustus the Fourth. The ram stared back in royal disdain of the whole affair. The beat of the helicopter overhead reminded them that each minute passing was an extra indictment against them.

'It might help, Judge,' Michael O'Reilly said gravely. 'Kelly's got a way with her.'

'Anything's worth a try,' the judge nodded. 'Not that I expect any success.'

'It's the only thing that's fair now,' Kelly said. She was nervously aware that the kind of petitioning she was about to do needed every advantage she could think of. 'I'm going to shower and change,' she said, cementing the decision.

Nevertheless, uncertainties churned through her as she stripped off her riding clothes and hurried into the bathroom. She remembered Justin's pride. He wouldn't have her marry him because of the horses. How would he react to an offer to marry him because of a ram?

She felt faint at the thought that he might very well spurn her. And his anger might then rebound on her grandfather and the judge.

But what else could she do? If her grandfather was sent to gaol, it would kill him. And the judge and Arlene Moffat would suffer such dreadful humiliation if they were caught in what they had done.

Kelly had to save them if she could. The only power she had over Justin St John was the power of her attraction to him. He did want her. She was certain of that. But, if he scorned to marry her, what could she do then?

Her heart beat more rapidly as she realised the full import of what she was thinking.

But it wasn't really like that! Kelly frantically argued the point over with herself. It wasn't as if Justin St John meant nothing to her. And he certainly wasn't repulsive to her.

He had spoken the truth this afternoon. If they had been somewhere else, somewhere private, she wouldn't have stopped him from making love to her. Because that was what she wanted. She had excused herself before with the tenuous argument that it was in the heat of the moment. But that wasn't the full truth. Self-honesty demanded she face it.

A shiver ran over Kelly's skin as she stepped from the shower. She dried herself vigorously with a towel in a futile attempt to wipe away her physical self-consciousness. It was impossible. Her body played traitor, remembering the sensations, the wanton desire that Justin St John had aroused. The moral dilemma in her conscience exploded into nothingness with the full blast of self-revelation.

She wanted Justin St John. She wanted to live with him, to sleep with him, to love him, to have his children, to please him and to take her pleasure from him. And damn everything else! Whatever the age difference, however much he tried to reject what she could give him, she would be her own woman! Together with him, joined in love, it had to be right. He wanted it as much as she did.

She and Justin could overcome anything. Go on forever. They were soul-mates. Hadn't she felt it from the beginning? Something bound them together, and it would always be so... had to be so... across the total span of time.

CHAPTER ELEVEN

THE WALK up to Marian Park seemed longer than Kelly had ever remembered it. But she needed the time to think and bring her emotions under control. She had no problem passing through the cordon of men surrounding the property. What would happen when she reached the house became her main concern.

She tried to swallow her apprehension and devise some plan. If Justin didn't want to see her, what was she going to do? And if he did see her, the same question had to be answered. What was the best way to go about it? The closer she got to the house, the more daunting her task seemed to become.

This was going to be very much an *ad hoc* affair. She would have to float with the tide, see where it was taking her, adjust to whatever circumstances arose and seize any advantage she could. Her heart pounded one refrain over and over again, drowning out everything else. This afternoon she had been a fool. She had to reach Justin and never let him go again!

Roy Farley was in conversation with a number of hard-faced officials at the front steps of the house. He frowned at her appearance, but the way his eyes rolled over the curves of her body was more than flattering. Kelly hoped that the embroidered camisole top that she had teamed with her best white slacks was not too revealing of her intentions.

'Can I do anything for you, Miss Hanrahan?' Roy Farley asked. His manner was distinctly wary.

'I wish to see Mr St John,' she replied, her eyes challenging him with determined purpose. 'I know he must be very busy, but this is important.'

He hesitated, frowned again, and finally shrugged. 'He's in the drawing-room. Do you want me to announce your arrival?'

'It's all right. I can do that myself,' Kelly returned quickly, not wanting Justin to have any advance warning.

She hurried up the steps before Roy Farley could have second thoughts. Both the front doors stood open. Only the foyer to cross. Nothing could stop her now. It had all been much easier than she had anticipated. She prayed that Justin was alone. But even if he wasn't, he couldn't refuse to see her when she was right in front of him.

One of the doors into the drawing-room was slightly ajar. Kelly pushed it open without knocking. Her sense of urgency was too overwhelming for such niceties to mean anything. She stood in the doorway, her eyes seeking and finding Justin instantly.

He was seated on the sofa that faced the fireplace. His body was in a pose of total relaxation: legs stretched out in front of him, his head slumped back against the cushions, a drink of some kind nursed in one hand. He had not heard the door being opened. Nor did he sense Kelly's presence. He was staring at Noni's portrait. And the expression on his face...

The purpose that had driven Kelly here—to this place and this man and this moment in time—quivered into uncertainty as a tidal wave of insight crashed through her mind.

Noni...

The sadness etched deep into every line of Justin's face, and his eyes—the naked look of yearning for something forever lost, of hunger that could never be satisfied...

The revelation shook Kelly to the depths of her being as she tried to fathom all its implications.

Justin had loved Noni. Kelly was sure of it. It answered so much that she hadn't understood. Justin's unreasonable prejudice against show-jumping, his aversion to Rasputin—a black stallion—the kind that Noni had ridden, to her death.

It was why he had bought Marian Park and changed nothing, neither the staff nor the furnishings or anything else; nothing but the show-jumping.

Noni and Justin—they had been the same age; Justin playing polo—their interests locked in similar pursuits; Noni so beautiful—Justin so devastatingly attractive. They had shared so much sixteen years ago.

And Kelly a child—a child so young that to Justin she had only been remembered as Michael O'Reilly's granddaughter.

The years pressed down on her like a suffocating weight. Justin had lived and loved and known it all before Kelly had barely begun her life. And yet that didn't make what she felt for him any less real. Nor what he felt for her. The past was the past. They had to grasp the present and make the future!

Kelly trembled slightly from the force of mind she had to exert in order to quell her uncertainties. She slowly shut the door behind her.

Justin's head snapped around. The next instant he was on his feet, his body tense, his gaze raking her, taking in every detail of her appearance before looking her straight in the face. The glitter in his eyes radiated a bitter cynicism.

'What do you want?'

She flushed at the mocking taunt, but refused to let it sway her. 'I've changed my mind, Justin. I didn't know it this afternoon. But now I do.'

His mouth curled. 'You've had time to think of all I can offer you. You disappoint me, Kelly. I preferred it when you were honest and said "no".'

'That's a terrible thing to say!' Kelly cried, hurt by his accusation. 'I might be a fool for not recognising my own feelings, but I've always played straight with you.'

'You mean that you haven't thought of the wealth and the position I can give you, Kelly?' he said sardonically.

She slowly shook her head. 'I thought only of us.'

He stared at her and Kelly held his gaze with unflinching directness, compelling him to accept her sincerity. And for several moments only she and he existed, with the future a shimmering mirage of possibilities between them. Then, with a flicker of regret, his eyes wavered away from the promise in hers.

'I've had time to think, too,' he said wearily.

'Of Noni?' No more secrets, Kelly thought savagely. Let everything come out into the open where I can fight it. 'You loved her, didn't you?'

His face tightened. Kelly could feel him closing himself off from her, and almost panicked. Had she been too blunt? Was it foolish to remind him of someone else when she desperately wanted him to concentrate on her... on them... the togetherness they could have?

Minutes seemed to drag by. Kelly didn't think Justin was going to answer her. She almost didn't want him to. Yet his very silence was a wedge between them, making any true understanding impossible to reach.

Finally he spoke with cold, hard deliberation. 'Yes, I loved Noni Lloyd. With all the passion that a man is capable of. I couldn't replace her.'

A terrible hollowness burrowed through Kelly's heart. Tears of sadness blurred her eyes: sadness for herself, for Justin, for Noni... for the hopelessness of it all.

'No matter how much you wanted me to be her, I couldn't,' she said in anguished despair. 'I'll always be me.'

It seemed to jolt him. His expression darkened. 'Is that what you think I want?'

Kelly's mind whirled again, grasping wildly at threads of hope. 'I don't know what you want. But you can't say you don't feel passion with me, because it is there. I'm not mistaken about that.'

He gave a harsh, contemptuous laugh. Words exploded from his lips. 'Passion? You have no idea of the passion that has been driving me.'

'I want you to tell me!' Kelly challenged fiercely, driven to the edge of desperation by his seemingly callous dismissal. 'Tell me what you feel! This afternoon you said we had something special. You know we do. And I want you to tell me I'm not making some dreadful mistake!'

She started walking towards him, her hands stretched out in appeal, her heart thumping with the need to reach into him, claim him as her own. 'However much you try to hide from me, there's a bond that ties us together. I don't know why it is, but I feel it. It's your life and my life...intertwined.'

His face drained of all colour and his fingers dug into her shoulders, keeping her at arm's length. 'You feel that?' he demanded hoarsely. 'You really feel that?'

'Yes.'

His eyes probed hers, incredulous...pained... 'You know who I am?'

The question was strained through a gamut of emotions that made no sense to Kelly. 'Of course,' she answered.

'You remember me?'

The tortured, haunted look in his eyes frightened her. 'No...no...' she choked out. 'What do you mean?'

The coiled tension in him eased. He shut his eyes, expelled a long, shuddering breath, then opened his eyes to glittering slits. 'You don't know,' he said accusingly, and released her, his hands falling to his sides as he turned and walked over to the fireplace.

Kelly was shaking inside. 'Tell me!' she hurled after him. He couldn't withdraw now. Not having gone so far. She wouldn't let him, even though she felt dreadfully threatened by what had been left unsaid.

Justin's gaze swung back to her, and a terrible violence of feeling simmered in his eyes. His face was harsher than she had ever seen it, carved in angry bitterness.

'You shattered my life once, Kelly Hanrahan. I won't let you do it again. As much as you were unknowing and innocent then...you did it. And as much as you are unknowing and innocent now, I will not let you do it again.'

Kelly swallowed hard to fight down a wave of nausea. It couldn't be true...what he said. She wouldn't accept it. Couldn't. 'Please...explain!'

A grimness settled around his mouth. 'Sixteen years ago, you forced a choice on me that altered my existence. Why I did it I'll never know. And that's the bond we have—you and I—tied by destiny to a moment in time when I had to make a choice. And I didn't choose the woman I loved. I chose you.'

Kelly shook her head, stunned and bewildered by the hammering accusation. 'I don't understand!'

'Do you remember Noni Lloyd's accident?'

'Vaguely. Only vaguely. It was a long time afterwards before I realised she was dead. I saw her fall. And she didn't get up the way she always did. I ran to help her. There was a stranger and he...'

Her voice faltered. She looked fearfully into Justin St John's burning grey eyes.

'You were running...running on your little childish legs to help Noni,' he mocked savagely. 'The black stallion fell after it crashed into the wall. Noni was thrown and knocked unconscious. The horse had broken a leg. It was trying to struggle up. I didn't even see you until the last moment. You ran out from behind the fence-jump, not looking at the horse, crying out to Noni.'

The blood drained from Kelly's face. 'You were the man who pushed me away...' she whispered, her mind pummelled by a whole sequence of memories. The hands gripping her arms hard...being swept off her feet...falling...and the soft caress on her cheek as she cried...Grandpa picking her up, cuddling her, taking her home.

'You didn't see the danger,' Justin continued in a hard, driven voice. 'You were only a child. You would have been crushed...'

'As you picked me up, Noni's horse rolled on you,' Kelly realised with horror. 'Your hip and leg...'

'I was trying to protect Noni... until you got in the way.'

'And one of its hooves lashed out and killed her while you were pinned... rescuing me.'

'Yes,' he said, and his voice was drained of all expression as he added, 'Indirectly, you were responsible for her death.'

Kelly felt sick. Sick and faint and totally shattered by the dreadful revelation. Sheer anguish strangled any further words as the inexorable line of logic savaged her mind and heart. Justin had been unable to save Noni's life because he had chosen to save hers, crippling himself as he did so.

Too stricken to remain standing, Kelly stumbled to an armchair and dropped into it. She shook with nervous reaction as other memories cut into her consciousness.

Justin hadn't wanted to see her again after he'd realised who she was. The child... the child who had cost him too much already. That was what he had said just before she had asked him for the horses, before his vehement rejection of her riding them for show-jumping.

And she had blindly and stubbornly persisted; taking the black Hanoverian stallion that was so like the horse that had caused the tragedy. Justin had driven himself through pain in a desperate attempt to stop her, the child he had saved, who was wilfully taking the same path that had killed the woman he had loved. And lost, because of her.

All those afternoons he had watched her practising the jumps with the horses, how it must have tortured him! And today on Rasputin...the mistake in timing for the wall, and only the black stallion's great ability carrying them clear.

She lifted agonised eyes to the man who had paid so dearly for the choice he had made. 'I'm sorry, Justin. I never realised. You should have told me before. I won't jump again. Not when you've been so hurt by it.'

He exploded out of the haunted thrall that was woven around his face, twisting with violent rejection at her offer, his eyes stabbing her with furious frustration. 'You think that's what I want? Why I tell you this?'

Kelly flinched at the lash of his words.

He turned away with a gesture of contempt, hurling more words at her with passionate intensity. 'You're free, Kelly. Free of me. You don't owe me anything. Your life is your own to lead. To risk. To do as you please. As is your right.'

'No!' Kelly pushed herself to her feet and caught his arm to make him stand and face her. 'I want you, Justin. More than anything else I want you. Even that afternoon when we first met, I felt it. You felt it too.'

Conflicting emotions warred across his face. The grey eyes were shifting seas of terrible turbulence. His hand lifted and curled around her chin, clutching hard. 'Kelly, don't tempt me,' he commanded grimly. 'It's too easy for me to take what you offer. Believe me, we'd both pay far too much for it in the end.'

'You want me,' she argued, fighting for the future they could have together. 'You wanted me to marry you this afternoon,' she reminded him in desperate entreaty.

'I was mad to propose it,' he said vehemently. 'That first day... when I realised who you were... that you were the child I saved... I was drawn to you. There was an affinity. A sense of reparation being made for what had happened before. A woman to share my bed... give me the children I didn't have.' His mouth twisted with self-contempt. 'What a mockery of love! You saved me much embarrassment by refusing my proposal point-blank this afternoon. I don't want to go into it any further, Kelly. It's finished. I no longer care for you.'

'I don't believe that. You do care about me,' she said with passionate conviction. 'Why else would you have come to watch me ride? Why else give me everything I want? You indulge me all the time.'

He shook his head, his eyes bleak and tired now. 'It's all mixed up with the past. Let go, Kelly. Cut free. Be happy in your own way. On your own.'

'And what if my happiness lies with you, Justin?'

Something flickered in his eyes—hope? . . . desire?—but he ruthlessly closed it off. He forced a smile of dry irony. 'A passing fancy. You'll get over it. The young always do.'

'I'm the same age now as you were when you lost Noni. Look how long it's taken you to find someone else whom you want.'

'Enough!' he snapped at her, his control visibly slipping. 'Go home! Be grateful you've made a lucky escape.'

He wheeled away from her and strode towards the music-room.

'You're running away again!' Kelly threw after him, too pumped up to accept defeat.

He paused and sliced her a venomous look. 'Anyone who doesn't run from disaster is a fool! I won't take any more from you, Kelly Hanrahan. You've given me enough grief to last me a lifetime. Go and jump your horses. Kill yourself. Do whatever you like. I don't care. I won't care!'

He slammed the door behind him as he stalked out of the room.

But he did care. Kelly was in no doubt about that. And the freedom he flung at her was a false thing. She would never be free of him. Nor he of her.

Kelly shook herself out of any acceptance of his rejection and ran after him. She couldn't let him go. Not when he needed her so badly.

He wasn't in the music-room. But Kelly knew this house like the back of her hand. And she belonged here. This house, this place, Justin . . . they all needed her. She was certain of it.

She swept on through the banquet-room, past the office, and turned into the corridor which serviced the guest wing. He was there . . . almost at the door of the room where she had given him physio-therapy that first day.

'Justin . . .'

He turned a ravaged face as she flew towards him. 'No!' he cried, anguished by her persistence. He caught her and almost threw her against the wall, pinning her there away from him. 'Why must you torture me? Haven't I said it all?'

Tears welled up in Kelly's eyes, filling them with luminous appeal. 'I love you. I love you, Justin.'

He bent his head, shaking it as if trying to shake himself free of the burden those powerful words inflicted on him. 'Kelly . . .' Her name was an agonised rasp.

'Please . . .' she begged, too distraught to find any more words.

He dragged his head up, his face working with uncontrollable emotion. His eyes burned with the torment of hell. With a rapid violence of movement, he scooped her away from the wall, crushing her against him with one arm as he opened the bedroom door with the other. He whirled her inside, shut the door, and leaned back against it, breathing hard.

'This is madness!' he groaned.

'No,' Kelly breathed, careless of the conse-quences, knowing only that she had to take the crest of his temptation and ride it through all his defences to the heart of the man. She reached up and wound her arms around his neck. 'It's what you want...what I want,' she whispered.

'It's wrong...it's wrong. I've got to let you go...' The words panted from him in sharp bursts, but his hands were running over the curves of her hips, her waist, up to the underswell of her breasts and back again in a restless yearning to touch and possess.

Kelly kissed the frantic pulse at the base of his throat.

An inarticulate cry burst from his lips. His hands clawed through her hair, pulled her head back, and he gave in, his mouth taking hers with a feverish passion that could no longer be denied.

And with the exultation of this triumph Kelly responded with a wild fervour, wanting Justin to forget everything but her and here and now. She wanted to wipe out the memory of Noni, the pain of the past, the differences between them. She wanted this to be the best, the most satisfying, most fulfilling experience in Justin's life...her life...their life together.

She kissed him with all the hunger of her mind and heart and soul, and Justin was irrevocably lost in his need for her, drawn beyond all vestige of control to taste all she offered, to savour it, plunder it, take, know, feel, immerse himself in the wonder of her.

So many times when Kelly had given him physiotherapy, she had wanted to touch him, not in the limited way she had, but to run her hands over the fine muscular tone of his body with sensual pleasure, to explore the firm texture of his flesh, to feel its warmth, its power, its raw masculinity.

She wouldn't let him stop her now. Wouldn't let him stop anything. She slid her hand down to pluck open the buttons of his shirt, felt his chest heave under her touch, thrilled to the rise of his excitement.

He tore his mouth from hers, pulled off his shirt, then slowly, gently peeled her camisole top upwards, his hands capturing her breasts, cupping their tender fullness, softly fondling for several breathtaking moments before he finished removing the flimsy garment.

He pulled her back against him, cried something unintelligible at the first brush of her flesh against his, then crushed her to him in a fierce embrace, showering hot kisses across her hair, rubbing his cheek over their path.

Kelly raked her fingers down his back, tasted the warm skin of his shoulder, rubbed her breasts sensuously against his chest, gloried in their semi-nakedness ... man and woman.

Justin lifted her off her feet, carried her to the bed, dragged away her slacks and briefs, tossed her sandals aside. He looked down at her, touched her, his hand quivering across her flesh in hungry desire before he snatched it away to remove the rest of his clothes.

He came to her with all the tense urgency of his need, yet delayed the moment of ultimate intimacy, plunging both of them into a wild exploration of sensation, the heightening of every sensitivity of skin against skin, texture, taste, touch, smell, sliding from one exquisite pleasure into another until stimulation and response peaked at the screaming demand for the total merging of one with the other.

Kelly's whole body convulsed in spasms of melting ecstasy as Justin finally pushed inside her. In that moment she wondered why it was always referred to as a man's act of possession. She knew she possessed him. He was hers. And every full, warm thrust of him was a glorious confirmation that he belonged with her, in her, and the union could never be sundered now.

She felt the jerking spill of his climax, hugged him tightly as the last tension eased away, and held him inside her, melting around him, bonding forever.

He brushed his lips over the soft, ecstatic curve of hers. Their breaths mingled. Their mouths mingled. A sealing of utter oneness...peace... contentment...fulfilment of every promise there ever was in the mating of a man and a woman.

It was complete. They would always be together from this time onwards.

CHAPTER TWELVE

IT BEGAN as a small wisp of uncertainty, the nagging knowledge that something had been forgotten. Kelly lay in Justin's arms, reluctant to admit anything that might intrude on their wonderful intimacy.

All the barriers Justin had tried to erect between them had disintegrated in the heat of their passion for each other. He seemed to delight in holding her close to him, caressing her softly with his fingertips. It gave her the feeling that she was infinitely precious to him, a possession he would cherish forever. As she would cherish him.

She basked in that thought for many long, satisfying moments. The memory of what had initially prompted her visit to Marian Park filtered into her consciousness. It jolted Kelly out of her delicious languor.

Octavian Augustus the Fourth! That had been the real reason for her coming to Justin. Kelly was swamped by a terrible wave of confusion.

'When do you want to be married?'

Justin's voice was a murmur of deep satisfaction, thrilling Kelly on one level, but raising panic on another. She had to tell him about the ram, but if he misunderstood...

Her arms convulsively tightened around him. Her mind darted in all directions, driven by the need to hold Justin's confidence in her love. She had fought so hard. He had surrendered. Nothing must shake their understanding now.

'Justin...' Her mouth had gone so dry, she had to work some moisture into it. 'I want...I want you to come down and meet Grandpa,' she said, frantically postponing the moment of truth.

He kissed her hair. 'Is it so necessary to tell him straight away that we're getting married?' he murmured, no more inclined to interrupt the magic of their togetherness than she was.

Kelly's brain skimmed over the responses. She could say that they had found Octavian Augustus the Fourth wandering around Grandpa's property, that they had picked him up and were keeping him safe in the kitchen. That...

But she couldn't and wouldn't start her marriage to Justin by telling a lie! That was no foundation for trust and understanding.

Kelly braced herself with all the courage she could muster. 'Grandpa...Judge Moffat...they have a confession they want to make to you,' she said, desperately trying to slide into the sensitive subject as tactfully as possible.

It was not only her and Justin's relationship at stake, but also the future relationship between him and Grandpa and the judge and probably the whole community of Crooked Creek.

Justin lifted his head to look into her eyes with a softly quizzical expression. 'A confession? I don't understand. Does it have something to do with us?'

The hands running over her hips ceased their movement as he waited for her answer. Kelly's heart seemed to thump right up to her mouth. She held him a bit tighter.

'Justin, you're not going to believe this...' There was no good way of putting it. 'I think they will have to tell you themselves,' she said weakly.

His eyes sharpened with a flash of enlightenment. 'They wouldn't have——' The incredulous words clipped off with a dark frown. His chest heaved and fell. 'No! They couldn't! Kelly...' It was clear that he had leapt to the truth and didn't like the taste of it one bit.

'They didn't really steal him,' she rushed out. 'You mustn't think that, Justin.'

'But they've got him. Octavian Augustus the Fourth!' he stated grimly. 'Why?'

'It wasn't really stealing,' Kelly pleaded. 'Grandpa and Judge Moffat took him because of your deal with the Russians. They were going to ransom him back to you...well, not exactly ransom him...but kind of like Rasputin. Make you see reason...'

Justin's mouth thinned and Kelly plunged further into explanation, frantic to appease his wrath. 'Grandpa and the judge have been in the sheep business all their lives. They thought you were being very unpatriotic to sell our best bloodline to the

Russians through the ewes. They're old men, Justin. They didn't think straight. And when all the fuss started, they didn't know what to do. Their pride wouldn't let them back down. And they couldn't get Octavian Augustus away with the search going on . . .'

'So they sent you up here.'

The words were a stinging indictment and a murderous rage suffused his face. He wrenched himself away from her and was off the bed before Kelly could utter a protest. He towered over her, emanating all the ruthless power that Kelly had sensed in him on their first meeting. And it paralysed her, strangling any word she might have said, thwarting any move she might have made.

'Get your clothes on, Kelly,' he commanded with icy, blistering authority.

'No,' she croaked, driven out of her shock by the dire necessity to fight his judgement. 'You don't understand . . .'

He dragged her out of his bed and set her on her feet. 'I was right when I said I was a fool this afternoon,' he grated, his eyes mincing her into contemptible little pieces. 'Let's not labour the point.'

'But that's not how it is!' Kelly cried in desperate denial.

His face tightened against any plea. 'Don't waste your breath. Or any more time. Get dressed.'

He turned away from her, snatched up the telephone, and punched out some buttons. His curt order for his car to be brought up to the house forced Kelly into action. She gathered up her clothes and took them into the bathroom, momentarily defeated by his pointed admonition not to waste any more time.

Guilt weighed heavily upon her. She should have told him about Octavian Augustus the Fourth sooner... had the search called off... disposed of the problem that was costing so much time and effort and anxiety. It had been crowded out of her mind by other more urgent, more important matters. She had to make Justin understand that. But it was painfully obvious that he was not prepared to listen.

The probability was that, the more she tried to say, the worse the situation would become. The assumption he had leapt to seemed all too credible in the circumstances. She could only hope that Justin would not be able to reject the truth of what they had shared when he had more time to reflect on it.

Meanwhile, there was one thing she had to make clear so that he would not expend his fury on her grandfather and Judge Moffat.

He was dressed when she emerged from the bathroom. A mixture of antagonism and intense bitterness glared at her. Kelly's stomach heaved with nervous apprehension. No way would he let her near him again. Not in his present mood. How she was going to soften him she didn't know...

'Grandpa and Judge Moffat didn't send me up here, Justin,' she said as steadily as she could. 'I came because I . . . because I wanted to. They didn't think it was a good idea at all.'

'But you knew better,' he lashed at her. 'I give you full marks for persistence, Kelly. You stop at nothing when you want to win.'

The sting of his words goaded her into another appeal. 'Justin, I love you . . .'

His mouth twisted in savage mockery. 'Don't worry. I'll serve your purpose. And then you can serve mine.'

Kelly flinched at the hard contempt in his voice. 'I never . . .'

'The car is waiting. And so is your grandfather. Not to mention everyone else who is engaged on a futile and misleading search. We'll have time for more words later. The rest of our lives together.'

He opened the bedroom door and waved her out.

Kelly moved, aware that any more argument was useless. Whatever Justin thought now, at least he was granting her some intercession for her grandfather and Judge Moffat. And that gave her another chance to prove the sincerity of her feelings for him.

The car was waiting for them at the front steps. Kelly tensed as Justin spoke to Roy Farley, but he merely announced his intention to take her home. He did not even mention Octavian Augustus the Fourth. But, to Kelly's leaping apprehension, Justin's face was as pale and immobile as marble when he turned back to her and performed the courtesy of seeing her into the car.

The drive down to her grandfather's house was short in distance but long in dreadful silence. Kelly wanted to ask Justin his intentions, but the expression he wore was too forbidding. He had shut himself off from her before, but this time she felt there was a solid, unbreachable wall around him.

He parked the car beside Judge Moffat's. Anxious to get the worst over, Kelly leapt out and led the way up the veranda steps, down the hallway and into the kitchen. Justin St John followed in her footsteps. As they entered the room, her grandfather and Judge Moffat hastily pushed themselves to their feet. Their faces underwent a wild spectrum of expressions from startled surprise to embarrassed guilt, before settling into stubborn righteousness.

Octavian Augustus the Fourth looked up in mild interest at the sudden bustle of activity around him.

'Justin, I would like you to meet my grandfather...' Kelly began shakily.

Justin nodded curtly, not offering his hand.

'...and his good friend, Judge Moffat,' Kelly finished, shrivelling inside at Justin's unforgiving manner.

The judge cleared his throat, but Justin cut off any speech he might have made. 'It doesn't look as if Octavian Augustus the Fourth has come to any harm. I'll have something to say to you two gentlemen in due course.' His voice was dry and bitter, and didn't brook any argument. He turned to Kelly. 'The search must be called off immediately. Where is your telephone?'

'Just behind you.' She pointed to the wall beside the door where the instrument hung above a handy cupboard surface where messages could be written.

They all watched him lift the receiver down, fearfully wondering what explanation he would give for the ram's presence in Michael O'Reilly's kitchen.

He dialled the number with sharp, incisive movements. It gave the impression he would gladly have jabbed the telephone through the wall. He rapped out instructions with machine-gun rapidity. He made no elaboration on the flat statement that Octavian Augustus the Fourth had been found. The ram would be held at Michael O'Reilly's home until collection could be arranged. The whys and wherefores were not entered into.

He put down the telephone and turned around, a cold, merciless pride stamped on his face. His eyes sliced at all three of them. 'Well, it's a fine conspiracy we have here,' he said in a biting tone. 'Two old men hiding behind a girl.'

The judge's face went red. 'That's preposterous...' he blustered.

'Kelly didn't know a thing about it until she came home from Dapto,' her grandfather interrupted strongly. 'What we did, we did for ourselves. Because what you were doing was wrong. So don't you take it out on her. That ram belongs to this country. So does its progeny. Just because you own it . . .'

'The reason I'm involved with the foreign sheep breeding programme is entirely on humanitarian grounds,' Justin said with steely emphasis. 'It has the support of our government . . .'

'I'm against them, too.'

'Grandpa . . . please,' Kelly begged, recognising the truculent look on his face and desperate to stop him from stubbornly digging his own grave.

'Reckon we've done enough interfering, Michael,' the judge put in with hasty wisdom. 'If Mr St John takes back Octavian Augustus the Fourth, and that is the end of the matter . . .' he shot a hard, meaningful look at his friend ' . . . I'm ready to forgive and forget.'

'Ah . . . yes,' Michael O'Reilly murmured, and his face visibly brightened.

The hairs on the back of Kelly's neck prickled. She knew her grandfather and Judge Moffat too well not to sense some hidden understanding behind their words. Had they committed some other crazy mischief as well?

'I wouldn't be wanting to upset Kelly any more,' her grandfather said decisively. 'So I'll say no more. Even though there's a lot more I could say.'

'Thank you.' Justin sliced a mocking look at Kelly. 'I trust my future wife will keep you to your word.'

'Wife?' Judge Moffat echoed in bewilderment. Then his jaw dropped open as Justin slid his arm possessively around Kelly's shoulders.

To her intense mortification, Kelly blushed to the roots of her hair. In her emotional confusion at Justin's blunt announcement, she forgot all about her suspicion that the judge and her grandfather had been up to something else besides taking the ram.

'Kelly!' her grandfather squawked in horror. 'You can't marry a man for a sheep! Not even one like Octavian Augustus...'

'I'm not doing that, Grandpa,' she denied hotly.

He looked confused. 'You're not marrying him?'

'Yes, I am,' she corrected. 'I want to,' she added hurriedly as his face stormed into disapproval.

'I won't have it! I don't care what he does or who he is! I won't have you...you...' He glared at Justin St John as if he were the purveyor of all evil. Before more words came to mind, his expression of rank condemnation changed to one of searching suspicion. 'I know you. I never forget a face. I'm not too good at remembering names any more, but I've met you somewhere before. Where was it?'

'Sixteen years ago you accompanied Henry Lloyd to a hospital room,' Justin acknowledged, a bitter irony threading his voice. 'You came to thank me for saving your granddaughter's life.'

Michael O'Reilly looked thunderstruck. Judge Moffat shook his head as if the whole situation had got completely beyond him.

The charged silence was broken by the sound of vehicles arriving, doors slamming, footsteps pounding up the veranda steps.

'I'll handle this,' Justin stated with calm authority. 'It will be much better if you say nothing at all. Any of you.'

No one questioned his command. All three of them stood dumbly by as Justin effected Octavian Augustus the Fourth's recovery with a minimum of fuss. The ram was taken away. The men who had come departed. Whatever Justin told them apparently satisfied them. The case of the missing ram was closed.

'Well...uh...' the judge rumbled when Justin returned to the kitchen. 'I think I'd better be getting home. All's well that ends well. We must be philosophical about these matters. Leave these young people to their...uh...more private affairs.'

He shot a beetling look at his old friend. 'I'll come around on Monday night, Michael. For our chess game. You can keep me fully informed then.'

Michael O'Reilly's gaze flitted from Justin St John to Kelly and back again, his brow creased with worry. 'Yes. You go on, Judge,' he answered, too distracted to think about chess or anything else. The bombshell that Justin St John had thrown him was set to blow his world to smithereens.

Judge Moffat turned to the erstwhile enemy and swallowed some pride. 'I appreciate your...uh...forbearance, Mr St John. From your point of view, it must have been somewhat galling.'

'When next we meet, I hope it's under more auspicious circumstances,' Justin said drily.

'Certainly, certainly,' the judge concurred, and took his leave without more ado.

Her grandfather broke the silence that followed Judge Moffat's departure. 'Kelly...' His eyes probed hers with deep anxiety. 'Do you really want to marry this man?'

She looked at Justin, who stared back at her with hard intensity, challenging the love she had declared for him.

'Yes. Yes, I do, Grandpa,' she said firmly. 'More than I've ever wanted anything.'

'Kelly...!'

Her grandfather's distraught cry drew her gaze back to him. He was shaking his head in despair. He heaved a deep sigh and turned to Justin.

'I'm an old man. I'd like to see my granddaughter settled happily before I die. Will you make her happy?'

'If it's within my power. I'll give her what I can, Mr O'Reilly. But only Kelly can tell you if her happiness truly lies with me,' Justin answered circumspectly, then slowly added, 'I will never deliberately hurt her. It's far more likely that she will hurt me.'

'You loved Noni Lloyd,' her grandfather shot at him accusingly.

Justin's face tightened into cold hauteur. 'That's true.' He swept them both with a look of glittering bitterness. 'I'll leave you to dissect me in private. Goodnight.'

He was out of the kitchen and down the hallway before Kelly recovered enough from his exit line to fly after him.

'Justin . . .'

He halted on the veranda. 'You can give up the charade now, Kelly,' he said wearily. 'You've got what you want. Your grandfather won't come to any harm at my hand. Now be a good girl, and leave me alone.'

CHAPTER THIRTEEN

KELLY hesitated, tormented by the knowledge that she had pushed Justin through one hellish pressure after another today. He looked totally drained, his eyes bleak and lifeless, his face older than his years. The strong sense of purpose that had justified all her decisions wavered and fell.

No matter what emotions she had stirred in him, Kelly felt in that moment she had failed...would always fail to earn the pure, unfettered love he had given to Noni. The bond they shared was twisted, shadowed, tainted.

A feeling of utter helplessness flooded through her as she envisaged Justin returning to Marian Park, sitting in the drawing-room, staring at Noni's portrait with that aching look of loss and yearning.

'Leave me alone.' The words beat a tattoo of despair through Kelly's heart. She watched him turn away from her, his shoulders hunched against the insidious arrows that fortune had flung at him, his footsteps painfully uneven in his walk from the veranda to his car. He did not look back at her, not even when he settled into the driver's seat and started the engine, nor when he drove away...leaving her alone.

'Kelly...'

She couldn't reply to her grandfather's call. She felt drained, too...drained and broken and lost. There was no fight left in her...nothing. Her eyes followed the tail-lights of Justin's car. They seemed to glitter derisively at her as the wheels bumped along the rutted road to the gate.

An arm curved around her limp shoulders and squeezed. 'You really do love him, Kelly?' her grandfather asked gently.

'Yes...' it was a whisper of yearning, broken by a sigh of despair '...but he doesn't believe me, Grandpa.'

'Because of the ram?' came the gruff question. He swung her around to face him, his face deeply lined with urgent concern. 'Go after him, Kelly. Go after him and make him believe you.'

She stared up at him with empty eyes. 'I tried. I tried all I could. It wasn't...good enough, Grandpa.'

His fingers dug into her shoulders. 'You're not beaten. Do you hear me, Kelly? You've been thrown. That's all. And what you do when you're thrown? Get right back on that horse before either you or he has time to think about it. Now go after Justin St John and stamp your will on him before it's too late.'

'It is...too late.'

'No!' His gaze stabbed over her shoulder and his mouth curved with grim satisfaction. 'Old habits die hard. The judge shut the gate when he left. Your man has had to stop, Kelly. Go now. You can catch him if you run hard.'

He half propelled her down the veranda steps and Kelly stumbled into a run, her legs pushed along by a force that was beyond her control, gathering a headlong momentum that pounded with painful need...a frantic, hounding need that had no hope, yet would not be denied.

Justin's car was at a standstill. The gate looked a garish white in the headlights. Kelly didn't understand why Justin was still in the car, why he hadn't moved. Her heart was bursting. Each breath was a pant of agony. He would get out, any second now. He would open the gate and go...and she wouldn't reach him in time. The red tail-lights mocked her, but her legs kept churning on...closer...closer...

The car door swung slowly open. Justin's silhouette unfolded against it. He leaned against the car as if he needed support, as if all purpose had deserted him and he was trapped there motionless, neither moving forward nor retreating...a shadow without life or meaning.

'Justin...' Her cry was a thin, reedy sound, insubstantial, yet wafting on the stillness of the night, reaching him, twisting him around.

'Kelly...' His cry was hoarse, driven, tortured... 'Wait...wait...'

She did not have the breath, the strength to plead more, but he waited. He even took a step towards her as she half fell against the boot of the car in blind exhaustion.

'Listen...please listen to me,' she gasped, not knowing what to say, only knowing that he had waited and was giving her the chance to say something. Tears of desperation sprang into her eyes. Her throat burned as she dredged words from her heart and forced them out.

'Justin, I know you will only ever love Noni. I loved her, too. She was like a big sister to me...so warm and kind and always so much fun to be with. I missed her...very much...and while she'll always live in my heart, she's not here any more, Justin. And I am.'

The tears overflowed and trickled down her cheeks, but Kelly wasn't even aware of them. Her whole being was concentrated on the man who was her life.

'I love you,' she said in passionate entreaty. 'If I didn't love you, I wouldn't fight with you. I'd give in to everything you want. But I won't. It's wrong, what you're doing...the way you've let things affect you...'

Her breath was coming in chaotic sobs and Justin's face was only a blur, but the words kept spilling from her lips in a torrent of despairing appeal. 'When you held me in your arms tonight, that was real...wasn't it? You loved me...a little, didn't you? Enough to...to have something good with me, even though I'm not Noni...'

'Don't!' The cry was wrung from him, scraping through the mangle of doubts that had entangled the truth. He lurched forward. His arms wrapped around her and held her tightly to him. 'Don't say that, Kelly. Don't ever say that again,' he implored huskily.

His voice was half muffled as he rubbed his face over the top of her head again and again. 'I did love Noni. I always will. She was everything you said she was and more... much more. But you, my darling girl... you are the life I want more than any other.'

Kelly barely heard the words. He was holding her, holding her as if he never wanted to let her go, and she burrowed her face into his shoulder, flung her arms around his waist, and clung as hard as she could.

He drew in a ragged breath. 'How can I explain it to you?' He sounded as desperate as she felt. His voice floated over her, strained with regret and hope and need. 'With Noni, love was a splendid discovery, a wonderful new dimension of life, and I took it for granted that it would go on forever. It was a shattering blow when she died. So this time... with you...' He gave a shuddering sigh. 'It frightens me... what I feel for you, Kelly. It's so deep, it ravages my soul. I've tried desperately hard to control it. To protect myself. To protect you. It's so terribly strong... the temptation to take you, keep you entirely to myself, hold you safe from anything that might take you away from me. I have to keep fighting it.'

He pulled slightly away to cup her face with infinite tenderness. 'I know I would stifle all your joy in life if I did that. And I love your joy, your courage, your unbounded spirit, Kelly. I love what you are...all that you are...too much to change one part of it.'

'You...love...me?' she whispered, still too torn by her own emotions to give full credit to his.

'With all the depth and breadth of life itself,' he answered, his voice heavy with resignation. 'There's no escaping it for me, Kelly. It's driving me insane. Whatever you do, whatever you want, I can't do anything else but love you. You're part of me now. Perhaps it was always meant to be...a little child that I had to save. I don't know. I think...sometimes... I don't know anything any more...except...I love you.'

'Oh, Justin,' Kelly breathed ecstatically. 'Keep on loving me. Keep on loving me forever.' And she reached up to press the deep fervour of her own love into a kiss that would leave no doubt as to her feelings for him.

He responded, because he could not help but respond, and they kissed and kissed again, hungry for repeated confirmation of their commitment to each other. Time was a meaningless swirl as they recaptured the closeness they had shared all too briefly at Marian Park, and with their uncertainties banished forever, the sense of togetherness was even more magical, more intoxicating, more fulfilling in every way.

'You will risk your life with me, Kelly?' Justin asked, wanting to hear the words.

She laughed in sheer happiness. 'Just try and get away from me, Justin St John. I'd fight you every step of the way.'

He laughed too, a deep rumble of pleasure. 'That I can believe. I shall try not to engage you in battle. You always win anyway.'

'Mmm...' Her eyes wickedly teased him. 'I think I can be seduced. You're a terribly distracting man. You've got no idea how hard it was to concentrate on giving you physiotherapy.'

He grinned, and Kelly decided in that instant that he was the most handsome man in the whole world... handsome and beautiful and wonderful, and all of him miraculously hers!

'No idea?' he scoffed laughingly. 'I doubt that your concentration was as difficult to maintain as mine. Every time you touched me, I had to block out the urge to make love to you there and then, and to hell with the consequences.'

His hands ran down her body with savouring possessiveness. 'And every time I watched you ride, I wanted to drag you off the horse and kiss you until you were senseless with wanting me and nothing else.'

Kelly sobered as she remembered the torment she had given him. 'I won't go show-jumping again, Justin.'

'Yes, you will,' he retorted determinedly. 'You loved taking those jumps on Rasputin this afternoon. And I won't make a prison of our marriage, Kelly. Your pleasure will be mine. And if ever we get my leg right again, I'll go riding with you. Be damned if I'll let fear dictate our lives. We'll do everything together.'

She smiled her delight up at him. 'Well, I'm certainly going to keep working on that leg...in between the times when you simply must make love to me. But as for the rest, I'm going to be very busy having babies, Justin. I always planned on having lots of children once I got married.'

He raised a slightly sceptical eyebrow. 'You did, did you?'

'Yes. And if I have to fight you for them, I will.'

His eyes sparkled with anticipation. 'I think I can be seduced. I rather fancy a lot of children myself.'

Kelly glowed with her love for him. 'We'll have polo players and show-jumpers and sheep breeders, and...' An idea struck her. 'You know what, Justin? I think Rasputin would make as great a sire as Octavian Augustus the Fourth. If I mate him with Rapunzel...'

Justin laughed, and Kelly thought what a wonderful, free, rippling sound it was. She had not heard him really laugh until tonight. She vowed to make him laugh more often.

He hugged her close. 'I love you more than I'll ever be able to tell you,' he said on a deep sigh of contentment.

She hugged him even tighter. 'I'll remember this moment all the days of my life,' she breathed happily. 'I didn't know what bound me to you, but now I do. It was the promise of what love could be. I'll always love you, Justin.'

And once more they kissed, losing themselves in each other, celebrating the joy of becoming one in mind and heart and spirit.

CHAPTER FOURTEEN

THEY were married a month later.

Despite Justin's misgivings, Kelly blithely withdrew from pursuing her chances as a competitor in the World Cup. She was far too busy to want to go show-jumping. There were preparations for the wedding, a honeymoon to be planned, clothes to buy and Justin's family to meet. And, as much as she loved riding Rasputin, that love came a very poor second to spending every available moment with the man who had only to look at her to send her heart soaring with happiness.

The St John family was delighted that Justin had finally found a woman he wanted to marry, and if any one of them held some reservation about the age difference between the prospective bride and groom, a few minutes' observation of their radiant delight in each other was enough to dispel any doubt about the wisdom of their marriage.

The wedding was held on the terraced lawns at Marian Park. The magnificent gardens were in summer bloom. The day scintillated with sunshine and benevolence from all who gathered to witness the nuptial celebrations. Justin's guests were mightily complemented by every man, woman and child who had any claim to belonging to the

Crooked Creek community. It was the most festive occasion that anyone in the district could remember.

Judge Moffat performed the ceremony.

He had rehearsed every line of the marriage service with his wife, perfecting the proper resonance of every phrase, sharpening every nuance of the words to give each its full measure of meaning and importance. Everyone from Crooked Creek thought he gave a grand rendition of the traditional lines that joined Kelly Hanrahan and Justin St John as man and wife in the eyes of God and all His creation.

It was the very popular opinion that Kelly had done them all proud, marrying the new owner of Marian Park. She was one of them. And she would make Justin St John one of them. It would be like Henry Lloyd's time all over again.

Their congratulations to the bride and groom resounded with sincerity.

Kelly looked heart-wrenchingly beautiful in her bridal gown and veil. And Justin St John was not a bad-looking man either, even though he was a good few years older than her. The general opinion was that he scrubbed up very well. A fine fellow. And no doubt about him thinking the world shone out of Kelly. He couldn't keep his eyes off her.

'A fine wedding!' Judge Moffat proclaimed afterwards to the grandfather of the bride, his voice honed to a rich roll by the demands of the day, his face more florid than usual from an accumulated consumption of the best French champagne.

'And he's a fine man,' his old friend asserted, nodding solemnly towards Justin St John. 'It's got me thinking... maybe we shouldn't have done it, Judge.'

'Now, Michael...' The judge eyed him gravely. 'We can't be mixing principles up with personalities. We did the right thing. All of Crooked Creek was agreed on it. And what's done is done. Anyway, the Russians will still get better than they'll ever produce naturally. Lambs that will grow the best wool the Russians have ever seen. No doubt about it. And we saved the best bloodline for our own country.'

'That's true, Judge. Guess I'm going soft in my old age.' A reminiscent grin spread over his face. 'We did plan it well, didn't we? Taking Octavian Augustus the Fourth to distract attention from the real operation. No one even thought of checking the cryogenic unit to see if the artificial insemination straws had been replaced.'

A smug chuckle issued from the judge's throat. 'Well, it was handy that Uncle Tom's nephew is the local vet.'

'Tom Kennedy sure was a slippery one in his day.'

'Heart's in the right place, though. Look after your own first. Can't go wrong doing that, Michael,' the judge said with wisdom.

'Yes, you can!' Michael O'Reilly protested heatedly. 'Kelly and that husband of hers won't leave me alone. Insisted I live up here at Marian

Park. Treating me like an old man who can't look after himself. That's wrong!'

'Well, Michael, you might as well face up to it. I reckon Kelly's got you beaten there.'

'It's a sad thing... a sad thing when a man has to leave his home of seventy years. But you're right. She's got me beaten.'

The judge searched for a way to cheer up his old friend. Inspiration came with a burst of triumph. 'Think of next spring, Michael! We'll be wearing smiles with every lamb born around Crooked Creek. Nothing beaten about that! We won. We may never be able to brag about it... except to ourselves... but we won!'

And that glorious thought brought broad smiles to their faces and they toasted each other with the best French champagne.

The months rolled by: summer into autumn, autumn into winter, winter into spring... and with the spring a child was born to Kelly and Justin St John. A son, whom they named Henry Lloyd. He had black hair, a dimple in his chin, and green eyes, and he promptly enslaved both parents for life.

It was not the only birth celebrated that spring.

On every sheep farm around Crooked Creek there was a fall of lambs that were remarkable for the fine quality of their wool. Lots of people wore very broad smiles. Octavian Augustus the Fourth was toasted as the prince of sires.

In the stables at Marian Park, Rapunzel gave birth to a black foal, who seemed to think that ordinary walking was a waste of time. He pranced and jumped and put Rasputin's nose out of joint with his competitive antics.

The seasons rolled into years that moved inexorably on to other years. Marian Park prospered...sheep stud...horse stud...and five children were born—Henry, Noni, Suzanne, Michael, and Christine—all fired with the desire to carry on the traditions that had grown up around their family home.

They gathered in the drawing-room each night after dinner to ask questions and be together. Even the baby of the family was included in this hour, although she invariably fell asleep on her great-grandfather's chest. He often fell asleep too, but Pa was very old, so nobody minded that. Everyone knew he was reserving his energy to outlive Judge Moffat.

'Daddy, who is the lady in the picture above the fireplace?' Michael asked one night.

'That's Noni Lloyd,' Justin answered quietly. 'Someone your mother and I loved very much,' he added, flicking a smile at his wife.

'She taught me how to ride,' Kelly put in.

'Why don't we have a picture of Mummy up there?' Michael said critically.

'Because no artist could paint a picture of your mother that was perfect, and we wouldn't be satisfied with less, would we?' Justin reasoned. 'We'd sit here and say, it doesn't show how her face lights up when she smiles, or the way her eyes grow warm when she gives you a cuddle, or all the things we see when we look at her.'

They all looked at her with such judgemental faces that Kelly laughed.

'You're right, Dad,' Henry declared. 'An artist wouldn't have a hope.'

'Tell us a story, Daddy,' Suzanne urged as she climbed on to his knee. 'The one when Mummy took Rasputin...'

'And you tried to stop her,' Michael crowed delightedly.

'And she jumped Rasputin bareback, right over the gate where you were standing,' Noni pressed eagerly.

'And eventually won the World Championship,' Henry added with filial pride.

'Go on, Dad,' they all urged.

Kelly rolled her eyes. Justin laughed. He had told the story so many times, the children knew it by heart, but somehow it never lost its magic for them.

'Well, you must remember that Rasputin was a real rogue in those days,' he started, frowning with worry as he was supposed to at this point. 'Not the placid old fellow we put out to graze now. No one could handle him...'

'Except Mum,' Henry put in with a wide grin. He was very much her son, and they shared a special rapport.

'That big black stallion was a mighty strong horse, with a will of its own,' Justin continued. 'And there was your mother, telling me he was a dream to ride. She was fighting mad that night, I can tell you...'

All the children grinned at that. Many a time they'd seen their mother fighting mad when they hadn't done what she'd told them. They could picture the scene perfectly.

The story went on, embellished by the children if Justin left out the slightest detail. Kelly watched her husband as he related it all again—tailoring it into the kind of story that legends are made of— yet there was so much more to it than he ever told...the emotions that had churned through them that night...the misunderstandings...their first kiss, which had been meant to frighten her but had turned into something completely different.

Their first kiss...

Her eyes softened with the love that had grown richer with every year. Her gaze swept slowly around their children—each one special in his or her own right—the future she had planned with Justin so long ago. And it had been all she had wished for and more. She sighed happily as she thought of the years still ahead of them.

Justin heard her sigh and glanced at her. Their eyes caught and locked, and for one heart-leaping moment there were only the two of them... together... discovering the bond again... and knowing the promise was true for all eternity.

And much later that night, Justin held her in his arms, caressing her body with featherlight fingertips. Kelly shivered with pleasure and hugged him closer. Justin kissed her hair.

'Kelly, I should have asked you...' he murmured. 'Would you like your portrait painted?'

She nestled her head contentedly over his heart. 'I liked your answer to the children better.'

'It's true, you know. Every time I look at you, there's more about you that I love. I don't want a portrait of you, Kelly. I want you.'

'I know,' she said. 'And the portrait of Noni belongs there, Justin. It's part of us, part of Marian Park...'

'Yes. Tonight I was remembering the first time I kissed you.'

'So was I.' Kelly smiled.

'At the time I thought... just this once.'

'Did you really?'

'Mmm. Very foolish thought.'

And he rolled her on to her back and set about kissing her again. Very thoroughly. And Kelly felt a great surge of love for this man who cherished her so much. So it would always be, she thought blissfully.

She remembered having once said that all life was a risk. And in a way it was true.

But not this part.

Not her love for Justin, or his for her.

That was rock-solid until the end of time.

Harlequin Presents

Coming Next Month

#1295 ONE MORE NIGHT Lindsay Armstrong
Evonne expected to be helping a young untried writer to organize and finish his book It was a favor to her employer Instead, Rick Emerson was a sophisticated, attractive, dangerous specimen who constantly disturbed her

#1296 MY DESTINY Rosemary Hammond
When detective Stephen Ryan made it clear he wanted to see more of her, Joanna remembered the last man she'd loved. Three years ago she'd been married to Ross, also a policeman, and he'd died in the line of duty Couldn't the same thing happen to Stephen?

#1297 FREE SPIRIT Penny Jordan
Hannah Maitland knew exactly what she wanted out of life, and men didn't rate very high on her list. She'd never been tempted away from her chosen path until she went to work for Silas Jeffreys.

#1298 A MOST UNSUITABLE WIFE Roberta Leigh
Her modeling career hadn't prepared her for child caring—but Lorraine was determined to care for her brother's children, orphaned by an accident. It wasn't easy—and her arrogant, authoritarian neighbor Jason Fletcher only added to her problems.

#1299 LOVE IS FOR THE LUCKY Susanne McCarthy
Ros had learned her lesson about men long ago and now kept her emotions firmly controlled. Then Jordan Griffin came on the scene tempting her to weaken—though she couldn't see why a famous rock star would be interested in her

#1300 RENDEZVOUS IN RIO Elizabeth Oldfield
Christa had been forced to leave Jefferson Barssi because of his arrogance and hard-heartedness. She and their son had been away from Brazil for six months. Now she was forced to return—and Jefferson didn't seem to have changed at all!

#1301 STEEL TIGER Kay Thorpe
Jan thought that Don Felipe de Rimados wanted a secretary Actually he wanted a son! She was attracted to him, but could she possibly comply with her unusual contract of employment—only to walk away afterward?

#1302 THREAT OF POSSESSION Sara Wood
Roxy Page was stunned when she inherited Carnock—after all, she was only the housekeeper's daughter Ethan Tremaine would go to any lengths to have the house back in the family, so she knew she'd have to be on guard against him.

**From America's favorite author
coming in September**

JANET DAILEY

For Bitter Or Worse

Out of print since 1979!

Reaching Cord seemed impossible. Bitter, still confined to a wheel-chair a year after the crash, he lashed out at everyone. Especially his wife.

"It would have been better if I hadn't been pulled from the plane wreck," he told her, and nothing Stacey did seemed to help.

Then Paula Hanson, a confident physiotherapist, arrived. She taunted Cord into helping himself, restoring his interest in living. Could she also make him and Stacey rediscover their early love?

Don't miss this collector's edition—last in a special three-book collection from Janet Dailey.

HARLEQUIN
American Romance

THE LOVES OF A CENTURY...

Join American Romance in a nostalgic look back at the Twentieth Century—at the lives and loves of American men and women from the turn-of-the-century to the dawn of the year 2000.

Journey through the decades from the dance halls of the 1900s to the discos of the seventies ... from Glenn Miller to the Beatles ... from Valentino to Newman ... from corset to miniskirt ... from beau to Significant Other.

Relive the moments ... recapture the memories.

Look now for the CENTURY OF AMERICAN ROMANCE series in Harlequin American Romance. In one of the four American Romance titles appearing each month, for the next twelve months, we'll take you back to a decade of the Twentieth Century, where you'll relive the years and rekindle the romance of days gone by.

Don't miss a day of the CENTURY OF AMERICAN ROMANCE.

A CENTURY OF
AMERICAN ROMANCE
1900's

The women...the men...the passions...
the memories....

CAR-1

THE LIVING WEST

Where men and women must be strong in both body and spirit; where the lessons of the past must be fully absorbed before the present can be understood; where the dramas of everyday lives are played out against a panoramic setting of sun, red earth, mountain and endless sky....

Harlequin Superromance is proud to present this powerful new trilogy by Suzanne Ellison, a veteran Superromance writer who has long possessed a passion for the West. Meet Joe Henderson, whose past haunts him—and his romance with Mandy Larkin; Tess Hamilton, who isn't sure she can make a life with modern-day pioneer Brady Trent, though she loves him desperately; and Clay Gann, who thinks the cultured Roberta Wheeler isn't quite woman enough to make it in the rugged West....

Please join us for HEART OF THE WEST (September 1990), SOUL OF THE WEST (October 1990) and SPIRIT OF THE WEST (November 1990) and see the West come alive!